THE
BLACK RECLUSE
BAD MOON RISING

Be sure to get your original copy of the classic rock song, "Prison Break" by the author Bill Passmore and David Passmore. Bill and his brother David formed the rock band, Smokey Jam. Prison Break was written about the James Earl Ray prison break of 1977. Purchase the song on Tunecore, iTunes, Apple, or buy the whole album/CD "Resurgence" – performed by the Smokey Jam Band.

THE BLACK RECLUSE

BAD MOON RISING

The true story turned to fiction account of J.R. Dawkins, aka the Black Recluse. A sickly, scrawny four-year-old boy, bitten repeatedly by a rare black recluse spider, which gives him a buzz that ultimately makes him crave the venom of this rare black beauty. He progressively gets stronger and more cunning throughout his days in a street gang, then the police force. After an incident that would have killed a normal man, the FBI turns him into their secret weapon against the most heinous crimes worldwide.

Author and Publisher, Bill Passmore

272 County Rd 587, Englewood, Tennessee 37329, 423-829-4831

Illustrations by Jesse Passmore

Cover and book design by Helen Mullins,

HM Graphics LLC, PO Box 398, Etowah, TN 37331, 423-263-7548

Printed in the U.S.A.

THE
BLACK RECLUSE
BAD MOON RISING

BILL
PASSMORE

THE FOUR-YEAR-OLD

A long time ago, in a small town in Tennessee, a brilliant black creature caught the eye of a four-year-old boy by flashing in the morning sun, then disappearing into an old, rusty water meter. Being very old, the meter's lid had broken away leaving a small crack in one side. Briars and weeds up to the boy's knees grew all around. This young boy was the inquisitive type, and nothing was going to stop him from finding this shiny, but elusive, mystery.

Making his way through the bushes and thorns, he used a stick to open the lid ever so slowly, making sure whatever he saw would stay inside that damp meter. As his eyes adjusted to the dark hole, he could see the rust and mud on the bottom and sides and, slowly, a web came into focus. His little heart was pounding in his chest. This discovery was something his excited little eyes had never seen before.

Leaning closer, he could see a set of weird looking eyes staring up at him. This jet-black creature with a rust colored violin shape on its back was beautiful to the child.

1

Hypnotized and drawn to whatever this creature was, the boy slowly moved his hands into the meter, trying hard not to displace the web. He slowly cupped his hands around this magnificent gem.

He worked his way up to the back porch where his mother kept her mason jars, and he placed it inside one of the tiny jars that had a lid on the top so that his prize could not get away. He was very proud of himself as he called for his mom to come see his find.

"J.R. Dawkins, what have you drug in this time," his mother asked in a harsh voice.

"Mama, this is the prettiest thing I've ever seen," he replied. "Well, let's see what's got you so worked up," she answered as the boy hands her the jar.

When she looked inside to see what he had captured, she let out a screech and dropped the jar.

"Oh, my lord, are you out of your mind? Don't you have any idea what this is?! I know you're only four, but you should have learned about bugs and snakes by now!" his mother screamed.

Luckily, the jar didn't break when it was dropped. She picked it up, stuck it in the boy's face, and said, "This pretty insect you have caught is a dangerous and very poisonous spider! It's a black recluse spider, and a large one at that! If it bit you, it could make you extremely sick, and that's if it didn't kill you first!"

The little boy was disappointed at what his mother had said. "But mom, it likes me, and I want to keep it," he said in a pleading voice.

"No, no, no," she firmly stated.

That's when she noticed his hand was red and a little swollen.

"Oh, my lord, let me see that hand," she said to him.

He slowly gave her his little hand, and she nearly fainted. "You have been bitten, son! We've got to get you to the doctor," she moaned.

She grabbed her purse and car keys and then she and her son were off to the family doctor.

The boy kept looking at her trying to understand what all the fuss was about. Then he noticed she had brought the mason jar with her.

In that little town, there was a couple of doctors, and that was about all. No fancy equipment, no special training — just small-town medical facilities. At that time, penicillin hadn't even been discovered, and the Sulfa drug was about the strongest antibiotic in use. That was saying a lot.

As she pulled into the small, brick hospital's parking lot, Mrs. Dawkins hurried her son through the entrance and yelled for a nurse or an assistant. Having neither on duty, the old doctor stuck his head out of his office and yelled, "I'll be with you in a minute, lady. I'm with a patient."

In panic mode, she pulled the boy to the door, entered, and startled the old doc and his patient.

"My son's been bitten by a black recluse spider, and he needs something now," she exclaimed.

As he stepped away from his patient, the doctor said, "Let me see."

He asked for the boy's hand and examined it.

Doc said, "Hum, hum... he doesn't act like someone that has just been bitten by a poisonous insect."

He questioned the mother, whom he knew as someone that had a tendency to overexaggerate things. "Are you sure it was poisonous?"

In a loud, exasperated voice as she handed him the jar, she said, "Yes!"

Doc admitted, "Damned if it ain't."

He began to examine the boy: blood pressure, heart rate, temperature, etc. Through all of this, the boy sat calmly, not saying anything.

Afraid he was in trouble and still wondering what all the fuss was about, he finally told the doctor, "I'm all right."

As he looked into the boy's eyes, Doc said, "You think so, huh? I'll be the judge of that, young man."

After looking him over from head to toe, Doc told the mother, "I'm going to give him a shot of Sulfa drug and some antihistamines. That's the best I've got."

Frantically, she whispered, "Will it save my boy?" That was when he told Mrs. Dawkins to step away from her son and into the next room. She followed him thinking, "something must be bad wrong!"

"What is the matter, doctor?" she asked.

"Ma'am, I've never seen anything quite like this. All his vitals are normal. Just a little bit of swelling is the worst thing he is dealing with," the doctor explained.

Relieved but still rationalizing, Mrs. Dawkins said, "Maybe the spider didn't inject very much venom when it bit him."

That was when the old doctor sat down, looked at her with a strange look, and said, "Lady, that black recluse bit him at least eight times on both hands. He should be dead or dying. My prognosis, for reasons I'm really not sure of, is the boy has a natural immunity from that black devil's venom."

Shocked, Mrs. Dawkins asked, "Then why is he so attracted to that creature?"

J.R. was a scrawny child, and not very healthy. He was very shy, and being the only kid, he played by himself with imaginary friends. When the spider bit him and injected its venom into his blood stream, J.R. felt such a high — a rush he had never experienced. It made him feel so "alive" that his little brain started manipulating information and analyzing details that no four-year-old should even notice.

On their way home, J.R. asked, "Did you keep the spider?"

His mother replied, "Yes, I have it. I had to get it out of the doctor's office, but I will dispose of it as soon as we get to the house."

She was so thankful that her little boy was alright, and she didn't want to make him feel as if he had done something wrong. J.R.'s mom loved him dearly, and he sensed her sympathy. As pitifully as he could, he asked her if he could keep the spider as a reminder to be more cautious around bugs. He promised to keep it safely in the jar.

At first, his mother objected, but after J.R. pleaded tearfully, she gave in. "Promise me you won't do anything stupid with that thing," she begged.

J.R.'s little mind was churning. Had the venom worked on him psychologically, making him more mature in his thinking?

They arrived home about six, and J.R.'s mom went to the kitchen to figure out what to cook for supper. She set the jar on a small table in the living room and reminded J.R., once again, to be careful with that devil thing. "Okay, Mom," he said as he skipped to his bedroom smiling and happy.

Later that night, after everyone else was asleep, J.R. laid in his bed, took the top off the jar, and let the black recluse crawl onto his little hand. His heart was racing, and his eyes were as big as a hoot owl. Slowly, he provoked the spider and felt its fangs penetrate his soft skin. Instantly, he felt the rush explode into his brain. It was four in the morning before he could go to sleep.

Over the next few days, J.R. scoured all the surroundings of his very large yard looking for more of these elusive spiders. Since the first spider was hiding in that rusty meter, he began looking in areas that were comparable. He caught two brown recluse spiders between the logs on a woodpile. Their venom was similar to the spider he had first cap-tured, but the black recluse had stronger venom and was very rare. This time he hid the two spiders from his parents. Now, he had three to let bite him, and he was so happy.

As days turned to weeks, and weeks into months, J.R.'s little muscles began to grow. He was running faster than he ever could before, and his intelligence had increased. He could reason at the level of someone who was ten. His parents saw these changes but were only happy about it. They thought he was just growing up to be a future genius athlete; they never questioned the reasons for the changes in their son.

As J.R. got older, the changes became more drastic in every way. Not only was he smarter and more muscular, but he was also more confident — even a little cocky. He was ruggedly handsome and had developed a mean, antagonizing personality, and he really liked the girls.

THE YOUNG TEEN YEARS

Growing up in the same small town with J.R. Dawkins, my best friend, Bob, and I knew J.R. We were good friends even though he was three years older. We also attended the same schools. Actually, we did just about everything together. We were as close as blood kin.

Bob and I intermingled with J.R. and his buddies quite often. We knew just about everything he was involved with.

My father, Carmel Passmore, got me a pair of boxing gloves for Christmas one year, so Bob and I signed up with the boxing organizations around the area. Bob really took to the sport, and later became the state Golden Gloves Champion in his weight division. He was trained by the famous Ace Miller that also trained Big John Tate who won heavyweight champion of the world. I said all that to say this: J.R. Dawkins was a beast, even at an early age. He was naturally more muscular and faster than anybody his age around town. He always had this big, smirky grin on his face, and he was as mean as a rattlesnake. J.R. was a typical "bad boy"— ruggedly handsome with black, wavy hair. He was kind of like Elvis. He even played a broom and lip-synced "Don't Be Cruel" while rotating his hips just like The King. I guess you could say he was one of the first Elvis impersonators.

The girls would scream; they loved it as though Mr. Presley himself was in the building. He was good looking and sexy, and he took advantage of it every moment he could. He had his pick of the girls. I think back, wondering about where all the strength, looks, attitude and such came from. I do remember one very odd thing. He had an aquarium — not for fish — for dozens of recluse spiders. I always wondered, "What was the attraction?"

J.R. was constantly looking for more spiders, and at the time, I thought he was crazy. He would take some out of the tank and let them crawl on his hands and arms. One time, I noticed the spiders actually bit him, but it didn't seem to bother J.R. Actually, he seemed to enjoy it, like he needed the poison. He would just give me that grin and say, "Bill Passmore, do not tell anyone." I thought about this, and I decided it was a stimulant to him, like steroids to a weightlifter. As wild as it sounds, it had to be why he was so tough. And he was addicted!

While I was in high school, hot rods, chopper motorcycles, duck-tail hairdos, and rock and roll were happening. "Dirty dancing" became a young people craze. I thought parents were going to have seizures! I'm sure you've heard the history of what people said about Elvis (The Pelvis) Presley.

Drive-in restaurants (like on the sitcom *Happy Days*) with good-looking girls who came to your vehicle to take your order were popular. This was where everyone hung out. High schoolers, college kids, motorcycle riders, and, yeah, hot rod owners, too. Man, did we have some good drag races.

J.R. and some of his bad boy buddies formed a street gang called the Turkey Dolls. They would show up at town events and start a rumble with anyone, especially fans from any opposing football team.

I was playing with my band at the National Guard Armory one Saturday night with a large crowd in attendance. People from surrounding towns were there, and one big ole boy was mouthing off something fierce. Naturally, the Turkey Dolls showed up, and I knew where this night was going. This ole raw-boned country boy was trying to get a girl to dance, but she didn't want anything to do with him. After she turned him down three or four times, he got really hot and loud. I saw J.R. ease over, and they had words. Words that I couldn't hear, but I knew what was happening. After pushing each other, they headed for the door. His gang members, along with a bunch of Raw-Bone's friends, followed. Half the crowd went to watch, too. I called for a band break and followed. I didn't want to miss the sideshow either. In the middle of this crowd, J.R. and Raw-Bone squared off.

I knew J.R. carried a switch blade knife and wore a chain around his waist. I breathed a sigh of relief when I saw it was just going to be a fist fight. I didn't want him to get into serious trouble.

The fight was on, and it had to go down as one of the greatest fist fights I have ever witnessed. I have seen, and even been in, quite a few. They swapped punches, like gamecocks in a battle to the death. It seemed as if it lasted for hours, but it actually only lasted minutes. It came down to the person that was the toughest and had the most endurance.

Finally, I could tell J.R. was wearing him down. At the end, ole Raw-Bone said, "I've had enough. You're a better man than me," and he turned and walked away.

As stated previously, I had witnessed one hell of a bare- knuckles street fight, and if I had only caught it on film, I could have sold it for big bucks to a fight

promoter. It was as good as any fight on TV or anywhere else.

Something strange hit me about that fight,
though. Ole Raw-Bone was gasping for air, but J.R.
wasn't even breathing hard. Mr. Dawkins was as wild
as a wolf and as cunning as a fox, but he had something else, too. I asked myself a lot back then, "What
did he possess that made him so noticeably different?"

All the Turkeys and their friends were cheering
and slapping J.R. on the back. He was the "champ" that
night. J.R. didn't say much, he just had that sinister grin
on his face.

One night, a car full of guys came cruising up
from a neighboring town to one of our many drive-in
restaurants. It just happened that J.R. was there that
night. Always looking for fun or a rumble, he spotted
the guys with the tags from a different county.
Walking up to the car, he gave a challenge to anyone
that would take him on. No one in the car would get
out, and I don't blame them. You might think four or
five men could gang up on him, but wearing a
leather jacket and motorcycle boots, they knew he
was a bad ass.

J.R. whipped off his chain-style belt and began
beating their car like a wild man. Starting on their
hood and then moving to their lights, he inflicted a
lot of damage to that car before they could even get
it in gear. They disappeared down the road to never

return. This was just one of the many crazy things he did, and yes, that grin followed.

A rebel's rebel, he was the most fun-seeking, mischievous kind of "outlaw" I ever knew. What really amazed me was how crazy the girls were about this rough boy.

There was a huge heavyweight boxer, older than J.R., that was making a name for himself — he was known as "The Bruiser." The local boxing club came up with the idea of matching this boxer and J.R. in a professional bout. There was a good amount of money that could be made because of their reputations.

J.R. wasn't afraid of nothing and said, "Let's go." It was set up at the same National Guard Armory I had played at earlier. A ring was built, advertising went out, and tickets went on sale. This was a big deal for little ole Kantrell Crossing, Tennessee.

When the fight started, The Bruiser looked like a giant next to J.R., but remember, J.R. was a Turkey Doll. The big dude charged him like a bull, swinging his hay-makers in a fury, but you can't hit someone that can move like Flash (the comic book character). Every time he swung, J.R. would move and counter punch. Float like a butterfly, sting like a bee, just like Cassius Clay (AKA Muhammad Ali). Pretty soon, J.R. was hammering him so fast and hard that his face was blood red and swelling. His eyes were taking a beating, too.

The fight lasted longer than I thought it would, but then again, The Bruiser was as mean and as tough as advertised. With a powerful blow to the gut, then a lightning fast left uppercut to the jaw, J.R. turned out the lights and sent The Bruiser to nappers house, good night! Again, I noticed J.R. was hardly sweating.

The fighters were paid, and J.R. bought himself a decent knock-around car, his first one ever. One evening, he pulled up to a small cafe downtown to grab a burger. As J.R. parked his car, a man he had a run in with earlier caught him with a knife through the open window. The man cut his face all the way down, barely missing his eye.

J.R. reacted by slamming the door into this guy, knocking him backwards, and as quick as a wink, he was on him and wrestling the knife from his hand, cutting it as he did. Then, with his fist, J.R. beat his attacker unconscious. Good thing the hospital was only a block away when the cops got there.

The attacker survived but was hospitalized for a couple of weeks because he had been beaten so badly. J.R. pleaded self-defense but was left with a deep scar on his face. He was never bothered by that character again, but his reputation was beginning to build up with the law.

I had a guitar player for a while that was one of the Turkey Dolls. He came up with a sound that was adopted by the gang. While shaping their hands like claws, placing them together, and then sticking them to their faces, they screeched like an owl, or something similar, but so much worse. It would agitate people, and it turned out to be feared by anyone that knew of them or had met them. When they all did it together, it sounded eerie. One of the rival gangs came out of the poorest place in Kantrell Crossing — a slum area that covered a large part of the west side of town called Tin Can Holler. It got the name because years earlier, people used it for a garbage dump, especially the metal cans that food, or most anything, was sold in.

Tin Can Holler was a rough part of town, but it was also a close-knit family type place. Fighting, incest, and even murder went on in the Holler. The girls were as rough as the boys. I witnessed many fights with the girls going toe to toe with the boys. You didn't want to date one of those girls.

I got into a fight with a Holler boy on the first day of my school life. He pushed me off the merry-go-round, and we wound up in the principal's office.

A book has even been written by a lady that was from the Holler called, *Tragedy in Tin Can Holler* by Rozetta Mowery, a must read with a lot of haunting history about that place.

THE GIRLFRIEND

J.R met this gorgeous looking girl from the Holler, and they fell hard for each other. Everyone kept asking, "Has the great J.R. met his match?" He was silly about her, so they moved into an apartment together. Everything was "honey" this and "darling" that.

When they picked the apartment, J.R. insisted that it had to be a three bedroom. One reason was that he liked to invite friends over to play pool, cards, or just party. He was always entertaining his guests with the Elvis thing, and the other spare bedroom was used for his workout equipment, etc.

His girlfriend, Brianna, worked at a small bank as a secretary/ teller, and J. R. was freelancing as a hot rod mechanic and motorcycle specialist.

At this point, he was bulging with muscles from working out and running. J.R. loved to climb trees, too, and he could go from the bottom of one to the top in a flash. Kind of reminded me of Tarzan!

One night, I asked him, "How much are you bench pressing?" When he said around 500 pounds, I knew he was probably telling the truth, at least this time. He'd been known to stretch things a little. I had been watching him change as he grew older, but there was something about these changes I couldn't put my finger on. It wasn't his body, but his personality and demeanor.

"Do you still keep those spiders?" I blurted out one day. With a strange look in his eyes, he pulled me up close by my shirt, and in a whisper said, "Don't you dare tell Bri anything about those spiders!"

"Hey bro, you know me better than that! So, has this become your little secret?" I asked.

"Yeah, I have over one hundred, and I've got them hid really good in my workout room. I can't live without them," J.R. said.

I thought to myself, "This is not human." Little did I know, it was just the tip of the iceberg. A year passed, and I kind of drifted away from the close brotherhood J.R. and I shared. I was busy doing hots rods and playing music with my band.

One night, J.R. showed up at a gig I was playing, and I hardly recognized him. He had grown a rough looking beard and looked twice as muscular as I had remembered. With a blank stare he said, "Man, I need to talk to you." Something was obviously wrong with my buddy.

"Sure thing, my man. It's good to see you," I assured him.

After the show, we went for breakfast, and that's when I found out he had really been struggling with something.

"Bri and I have been arguing a lot. She accidentally found my "secret" a while back, and she is freaking out," J.R. said.

"You mean those spiders," I replied.

"Yes, and she insists I explain why I have them. She knows something is going on that's not normal and gave me an ultimatum," he explained.

We talked about the situation for a long time, and I began to realize he didn't care for Brianna like he originally had. All of his thoughts and even his existence was centered around the spider venom that flowed through his veins. It was taking over his life.

"I haven't told anyone, but I've been bench pressing close to one thousand pounds," J.R. whispered. It all started to become clear to me what it was that was happening to my long-time friend.

"I'm not telling Bri anything except that our relationship is over. Will you help me get through this?" J.R. asked.

"If that's what you really want, yes," I replied.

With that assurance, J.R. parted ways with Brianna and decided to leave everything behind in Kantrell Crossing. He moved to Knoxville, Tennessee for a fresh start.

Not able to wrap my brain around all this information, I just laid back and tried putting all of these pieces that made no sense together. Though I knew I was dealing with something right out of the twilight zone. J.R. cared more for his spiders than this gorgeous woman — how was that even possible?

THE TURN AROUND

Three months later, J.R. had an apartment on the south side of Knoxville close to the Tennessee River. Built up on a bluff, he had a panoramic view of the city.

He applied for a job at a popular workout facility, and after one look at him from the manager, J.R. was hired. It was a definite no brainer. This was just what he needed. Pumping iron made him feel alive, and he soon became the top trainer. Everyone wanted him.

Some of the customers that came to work out were guys from the city police force. They all liked J.R., and he was beginning to develop a body like Charles Atlas, a top body builder at that time. The cops couldn't believe how much weight he lifted. Nobody could beat him in a weightlifting contest. J.R. had created quite a reputation for himself.

After investing in a nicer car, J.R. started making the night scenes around town. Word of him spread, and the women were in awe.

One popular night spot was named the Go-Go Club. The owner, Billy Sims, was also a weightlifter, so he and J.R. became friends. They began competing against each other. Billy then hired J.R. part-time to be the doorman or bouncer. This was right down his alley because he loved to fight, and it was legal this way. If anyone got out of line, he would punch them in the gut and then spray pepper spray in their face. Out the door they all landed, and it didn't matter how big or tough the person was. It was over in a moment.

Billy was always promoting his club with different kinds of schemes, and once, he had a giant boa constrictor painted all the way around the dance room wall. With black lights on, the wild colors of the snake came alive.

Somehow, Billy even bought an African lion cub that had been smuggled into the states. It weighed around fifty pounds at six months old and had paws as big as Billy's hand. He brought it to the club, and everyone went crazy over it. The lion would play with everyone; though it did bite pretty hard. J.R. was crazy about that lion. He would go to Billy's house during the day and play with that exotic animal. The two would creep up on each other and fight. Sadly, one night the lion jumped off Billy's porch, and, wearing a chain, hung himself. I don't know who was the most heartbroken — Billy or J.R.

Being around the guys on the police force often, J.R. became close friends with them. One day, one of the cops asked him, "Why don't you join the force? They are always looking for big- type men like you."

They all said they would give him a good recom- mendation, so, J.R. said, "Let me think about that."

A few weeks went by, and he kept running this idea through his mind. "I was a Turkey Doll street gang member — been in hot water with the law almost my whole life. I'm addicted to spider venom and hot women — many as I can get, both urges I can't seem to control," J.R. thought out loud.

As he reflected back to his younger days, J.R. re- alized that something had drawn him away from those days that he left behind in Kantrell Crossing. The love for adventure, for fighting, had grown even stronger. He had built himself into a muscular specimen that craved the unknown.

"Is this addiction I have driving me?" he won- dered. Then it hit him like a ton of bricks. "If I joined the police force, I could get paid for doing all the things I love to do. I would want to be a motorcycle cop, of course, and roam the city at night, though. I love the darkness, and it would be legal this time around," J.R. said out-loud. "Imagine that, Turkey Doll turned cop." The thought of "flying" around town on a

Harley Davidson and meeting danger head on was an overpowering adrenalin rush through him.

Right then and there, he committed to take their offer, and the next day, he contacted his police buddies to say, "I'm ready." With all those friends he made at the gym, it was no time at all until his application was approved, even though his background check had left a lot to be desired. That was conveniently overlooked, and soon, becoming a cop was a reality.

Black Recluse spiders are rare in nature and so was J.R. He had their venom flowing through his veins, so he determined that he was king of the "fiddle back," and this was a powerful driving force.

He told his superiors exactly what he wanted, which was to become a motorcycle policeman on a Harley Davidson with a Black Recluse decal on the windshield and helmet. He also wanted a long, white scarf to go with his black leather jacket. Then he told them, "I want to holster a forty-five-caliber pistol on one side and a sawed off, double barreled, pistol gripped, twelve-gauge shotgun on the other." Shockingly, they gave him what he asked for, and I've never understood why they bent the rules for him. I guess they knew he was something special.

His clothes were always pressed immaculately. His cycle was waxed so bright you could comb your hair in the paint job. The first time I saw him on duty, I was flabbergasted and proud of my ole buddy. Wow, what a transformation; what a sight!

J.R. had freedom to roam the city, and my band was performing in town. He knew our schedule and was waiting on us at the city limits. Turning on his blue lights, we fell in behind and got an eighty mile-per-hour escort to the club. We thought we were big time.

J.R., or the Black Recluse as he was becoming known as, was loving this new adventure in his life. He took to it like a pig to a mud hole. The first month, he was selected as the cop of the month for catching speeders, drug users, and such, which excited him more and more.

One night, he noticed a vehicle swerving, so he blue-lighted the driver, and all of a sudden, the car sped off. Falling in behind, he called for backup and pulled up beside the "runner." The car windows were tinted, but J.R. had developed vision stronger than that of a normal person. He could see that it was a man behind the wheel. Within seconds, the car (a 1960 Corvette) was up to one hundred miles an hour, but that didn't bother the Black Recluse. He was glued to the guy's bumper, and that long, white scarf he wore was flapping in the wind.

Suddenly, the Corvette made a quick turn down another street. The driver thought he could outmaneuver J.R. — WRONG! Turning right, then left at a high speed was nothing for J.R. He was laying that Harley almost on its side as the curvy chase proceeded.

All of a sudden, the driver turned down a dead-end street by mistake. As he slammed on his brakes and came to a stop, he looked up and was staring down the barrels of a twelve- gauge shotgun.

"Don't shoot," the man yelled.

J.R. grinned and said, "Why not? I'll just say you pulled a gun on me, and I blew your head off." The guy thought he was dead for sure, but J.R. was just having fun, so much so that the poor fellow pissed on himself.

All this dude had on him was a joint of marijuana, but he was running from a cop and endangering everyone on the streets.

As he put the guy in handcuffs, J.R. said, "By the way, tell all your buddies to never run from the Black Recluse."

The backup cops arrived, and the last thing the runner saw as he was placed in the back of a police car was that black, fiddle-backed spider on the motorcycle windshield.

J.R. was becoming the top cop in town. He was making more stops and arrests than any other policeman. In fact, he was always the cop of the month. J.R. was getting stronger and stronger with his workout routine at the gym also.

Mr. Dawkins had discovered a way to "milk" the venom from his spiders — a process similar to milking a snake. It was more concentrated and potent than a bite. After collecting the venom in a vial, he would keep it refrigerated and, using a needle and syringe, he would draw it out and give himself a shot in his leg. The same procedure people followed when they used steroids.

All the fellows at the gym couldn't help but notice how big he was. Discussing it among themselves, the only explanation they came up with was that J.R. was simply a freak of nature. They were partially right. He was going up in clothes size, and his desire for women was increasing. I, personally, knew what was happening, but I also knew he couldn't stop. I'm not sure how many people knew his secret, but he asked me to swear an oath that I wouldn't tell anyone. So, I kept my promise. Plus, I was a little intimidated by him. Who wouldn't be?

MOONSHINE RUNNERS

Back in those days, moonshine whiskey was a very big thing in the hills of Tennessee. "Shine" families would brew it, and hot shot drivers would deliver it to the Mississippi River, all the way across the state.

Usually, the drivers were the younger kin of a family that had stills hidden in the mountains. They were cream of the crop drivers and deliverers. Nothing was spared on the engines so that the drivers could outrun the police and "revenuers." Revenuers were agents of the U.S. Treasury Department, agents whose sole responsibility was to enforce the laws against illegal distilling or the bootlegging of alcohol.

The drivers bored and stroked oversized pistons, racing cams, super chargers, triple carburetors, etc. Most cars were plain looking Fords or Chevys, but they could literally fly. Those boys sure knew how to straighten out those mountain curves! Special tanks were made to go underneath the cars and be out of sight to haul the shine. The drivers knew every backroad and alleyway across the state. It was almost impossible to catch one, and it took one hell of a road-block to succeed. That was until the Harley-riding Black Recluse came on the scene.

Now just to give you an explanation of how good these drivers were, they would get together up in the hills on the right kind of road and have friendly races just to prove who was the best.

On a decided Sunday, they would meet, line up, and race around a designated course giving it every-thing they had from speeds of zero to one hundred and fifty miles per hour. Sometimes they wrecked, and sometimes, especially on a delivery, one would get killed. That was just a part of the life they knew.

The races were mainly a practice at outrunning the law. No one wanted to get caught and put in jail where they would be interrogated unmercifully. Not that one would ever break or give out any information about their moonshining operation. This is actually where Nascar racing came from. It had nothing to do with moonshine, but these races caught the eye of the racing world. It then started evolving into what we see at Daytona today.

J.R. was originally a street gang member and fighter. He drank moonshine and Jack Daniels to name just a few, but this part of his life had to slow way down when he became a cop. Eventually, he quit it all to-gether.

J.R. had heard that Knoxville was a route that a lot of moonshine runners used. In those days, there weren't as many policemen as there are today, and methods of communication weren't as ad-vanced either so runners were seldom apprehended. Just the thought of the challenge of catching one of these hot shot drivers was more than J.R. could stand. It excited him so much that he started study-ing everything he could get his hands on about these illegal money makers. He researched every road and cow trail in this part of the country.

With an uncanny photographic and manip-ulative mind, he soon figured out how and when the drivers formulated their routes. His calculations were more advanced than even the first computers could complete, and this was what he had always lived for. It was born in him.

After studying the pattern of one of the top drivers from the Smoky Mountains, J.R. set his "web." While explaining his idea to his superiors, he made a promise to be successful. He calculated that the moonshine driver would be using Kingston Pike in Knoxville as his main route to Memphis.

With his reputation, the superiors had no reason to doubt him, so they said yes, but you are on your own.

"If something goes wrong, we don't know anything about it," the police chief said. J.R. grinned and said, "What are you talkin' 'bout? I'm not even a figment of your imagination."

"You know what — you are about the craziest human being I've ever encountered. Get your ass back out there on that steel horse," the chief laughed.

"This is going to be wild," J.R. thought to himself. "Yes, what I live for," he yelled.

The day arrived that J.R. had calculated would be when the load of moonshine would come out of the mountains. As twilight crept across the hills of East Tennessee, the Black Recluse was hidden at a desolate crossroad where three seldom used roads came together. He knew which road would be the route back to Knoxville, so he eased back on his bike and patiently waited.

The mountains were full of shadows and eerie sounds. Overhead, the moon was almost full and with his vision — even more spider-like now — he could see the animals begin to stir. A deer wandered across the

27

road, and in the distance, the howl of a gray wolf ech-
oed through the hills.

"I hope that is a werewolf. I'm ready for anything," J.R. thought to himself. He was on the "hunt"
just like the wolf, and he was in his natural environ-
ment.

As the hours passed, J.R. realized his calculation
was slightly off, but his instincts said, "It's close." As
day broke, he went into survival mode. Faced with
this situation, he knew instinctively what to do. He
must wait until the next sunset.

With his cycle well hidden, J.R. went into the
woods until he smelled a rabbit. As cunning as a fox, he
moved into position and snagged the bunny with his
bare hands. He skinned the rabbit, cut the head and
feet off, then gutted the animal. After washing it in a
creek, he devoured the animal raw. "Not too bad," he
thought. After drinking all he needed from the creek,
he headed back to his motorcycle and found a comfortable spot to catch some shut eye. As he was sleeping, a couple of spiders crawled by, then a big timber
rattlesnake slithered close, but they all sensed something different about J.R. and crawled away quickly.

The next evening found J.R. on his cycle waiting patiently for his "prey." Not a single vehicle or
human had been by, but J.R. felt that someone was
coming.

Midnight came, and the Black Recluse was in
attack mode. One o'clock, then two o'clock, but by
three he heard the deep throated rumble of a mighty

engine with glass packed mufflers coming from up the mountain.

As he fired up his steel horse, his heart began pounding in his chest. J.R. threw his scarf back, adjusted the visor on his helmet, and with his gloved hands, rolled into pounce position.

"It doesn't get any better than this. We're about to see how good these shine boys can really drive," he said to himself.

Suddenly, out of the darkness, the bright, specially made headlights came into focus through the dust made by the slick tires on the back of that hot rod Ford. The car had blown by J.R. in a whirlwind.

"Oh yeah!" J.R. screamed. Hitting the throttle so hard that his motorcycle leapt forward on only the back wheel, the Black Recluse was in hot pursuit. It was a good half mile before the front tire levelled back off to the ground.

"Who is this Evil Knievel behind me? That moron is going to be hog meat," the Ford driver said to himself.

In an instant, the Black Recluse was inches from the car's bumper with the dust blowing underneath him. Around the sharp curves at a rate of speed that would have caused most drivers to wreck, the chase was on.

It didn't take shine boy long to realize he was up against something other than an ordinary cop. J.R.'s reflexes were quick as a lightning bolt. The driver couldn't shake him, so he decided to end the chase by slamming on his brakes. J.R. was too close, but he was able to whip the motorcycle to the side and go off the road into the woods. The Black Recluse zig-zagged through the trees with his gas gripped to the metal.

Thinking he had finished his pursuer off, the shine boy laughed and said out loud, "Ain't nobody that can run with the big dogs up here."
At that moment, J.R. jumped a hill of earth and came flying out of the trees and through the air. The hillbilly couldn't believe his eyes! Once again, he had a spider on his back.

As the dirt road turned into asphalt, the shine runner pushed his angry engine to its max. With Chuck Berry's "Oh Maybelline Why Can't You be True" playing in his mind, J.R. started singing while the Harley's engine screamed.

J.R. hadn't figured out how he wanted to bring this bad boy down. He really didn't want to kill him since he admired the driving skills of this guy. He decided his best course of action was to not give the runner anywhere or any way to hide so that, just maybe, the shine boy might give up and he could arrest the guy.

The chase was headed straight toward Knox County, and at the speed they were going, it wouldn't be long until they hit Knoxville. Since J.R. was on his own, no calls were made. They would soon be in K-Town. The two were so close to each other they looked as if they were connected.

Once they got close to town, the two were blowing by vehicles and driving down the streets in the wrong lane. Other drivers were hitting the ditch or running into yards and fields to keep from hitting them head-on.

J.R. admitted to himself, "This cat can flat out drive, but I'd better try bringing him in before we kill somebody."

Then he pulled up to the driver's side and showed his pistol. All that did was make the driver swerve into J.R., trying to crash the cycle. J.R.'s reflexes were too quick, and he dropped back behind him.

Soon they were on the west side of Knoxville. This was when intentions changed. The shine runner pulled a gun and fired several shots back toward J.R. to no avail. The spider's instincts are way too sharp.

That just agitated J.R, so he blew out both back tires with his .45, and at ninety miles an hour, the moonshine driver lost control and flipped the car, over and over. The "great" driver would drive no more. The wreck happened on Kingston Pike.

Do you remember the movie and song "Thunder Road", and what happened to the moonshine runner? The song lyrics go, "Right outside of Bearden, down on Kingston Pike, the devil got the moonshine and the mountain boy that night." They refer to the boy being killed by Revenuers, but now you know the real story!

OUTLAW BUSTER IVANS

There was a man that lived deep in the mountains who made moonshine and was involved in many other illegal endeavors. He poached black bear and all other animals that were protected by the wildlife agency. Hunting season for him was twelve months a year. He was a huge man and was as mean as they come. He had a reputation that included the death or disappearance of twelve men who had crossed his path. Everyone, including the law, was intimidated by Buster Ivans. He would kill anyone for any reason.

Now, this mean man lived in a little log house. He didn't own a car and didn't have running water. He used a well and an outside toilet or a "johnny." He had a wood-burning stove that he used to cook on and heat the place. Living off the land, he was considered an "outlaw."

Not owning a car, he would haul moonshine, furs, deer meat, ginseng, or whatever else he had to sell down to the closest town in a horse-drawn wagon. Buster would pull up to his favorite corner, set up shop, and sell his haul to the locals. Everyone knew him and knew as long as you didn't upset the man, you were his friend. The law would just pretend he wasn't there.

The state knew all about this bully, but they didn't know how to deal with the situation. He was always packing pistols and rifles, so the cops didn't think it was worth getting killed while trying to bring him down.

Word had gotten around the state about a motorcycle cop in Knoxville nicknamed The Black Recluse. A meeting was privately set up by the state department and the Knoxville police chief. They hashed over all the things J.R. had been doing, and agreed this man was definitely something special.

Once again, J.R. was in the chief's office but this time to discuss the Buster Ivans problem. He was told it would be an undercover job, and he would again be on his own. The police chief would deny having anything to do with it if things went south.

I think my ole buddy had so much spider venom flowing through his veins, he would have agreed to take on a pack of werewolves! Once again, that taunting grin spread over his face.

"When do you want me to hunt this animal down?" J.R. asked.

For the next couple of weeks, J.R. did nothing but collect all the info on this notorious outlaw that he could find. He studied Buster's habits, his routines, how long it took to brew his moonshine, and how often he brought it to town. J.R.'s plan was to locate his cabin and encounter him on his way to town so that no one would be in the crossfire.

A problem arose that J.R. discovered during his research. Buster didn't get away with all the things he did by himself. He had informants that were kin to him who were also in law positions. Word got back to Buster about the Black Recluse and what he was planning to do. So it wound up that neither was scared of the other and both were anticipating their meeting.

While J.R. was formulating a plan, so was Buster. He called on two of his meanest cousins to help set up a trap for this "spider." They would stay at Buster's cabin and then station themselves down the trail that led to town while Buster ran his next load.

Three days before Buster made the trip to town, the kin folk hid and camped out along the dusty path. They figured if they were set up before J.R. came, they could ambush him. If that didn't succeed, Buster was loaded for bear.

The outlaw made sure the town folk knew what day he would arrive. Since he made some of the best shine, the people were anxiously counting the days. This was also his plan to make sure that J.R. knew exactly when he would leave the cabin, but it raised a red flag in J.R.'s mind. This made it just too easy. Black recluses are leery, cunning, and the master at trapping prey, so the Black Recluse instinctively knew to stay alert.

The day came, and Buster left out around five o'clock in the morning from his mountain cabin. Everything in this outlaw's plan was in place. "That insect don't know who he's messing with," Buster growled to himself.

After injecting spider venom for years, J.R.'s vison, hearing, and sense of smell was supernaturally heightened to more than any normal human's.

J.R. had been calculating the encounter for days, just like a spider spinning its web. Instead of his well-known Harley, he chose a powerful dirt bike, and he had a muffler designed to replace the original, too. A police mechanic created a muffler that was completely silent, like a gun silencer. Now, Buster wouldn't hear J.R. coming, and with his super senses, he could detect if and where a human was hiding.

As J.R. started his ride up the mountain trail that Buster used, he was moving fast but made no sound. He wasn't sure how much help the outlaw had recruited, but he knew he could sense them before they would be able to see him.

About twenty miles up, J.R.'s built-in radar sent a signal to his brain that someone was not very far ahead. He turned into the woods and traveled through the trees and bushes to surprise the outlaw's cousin who was down in a ravine close to the trail. The ambusher had an automatic shotgun loaded with double-00 buckshot shells.

J.R. sensed he was getting close to his prey, so he stopped the bike and, quiet as a mouse, snuck up behind the man. His heart was pumping overtime from the adrenalin running through his veins. This was what he lived for.

With that smirky grin, J.R. said, "Good morning."

This caused the would-be shooter to nearly jump out of his skin. He swung around with his shotgun to blow J.R. into kingdom come, but that was the dumbest thing he could have done. Before he could turn all the way around, the shotgun slammed into J.R.'s hand. As J.R. jerked the shotgun out of the guy's hands, J.R. whacked him across the face with that sawed-off shotgun he carried in his free hand. When the guy came back to reality, he had him gagged and tied with ropes spread between the trees like a spider web. One down, and getting back on the trail, the Black Recluse continued.

Traveling silently up the road, thoughts flowed through J.R.'s mind about where he came from and where he is now. Never did he dream that he would be on this side of the law. He was born a "hell raiser," but somewhere along the way, his demeanor had changed. He had developed a good feeling about doing the right thing with his life. My ole buddy had definitely chosen a different outlook on his life, and I could definitely see it. Living was even more exciting to him now, and he thrived on this excitement — chasing down danger and all the shadowy things on this earth.

All of a sudden, the Black Recluse was pulled away from his thoughts by a flash of metal up ahead. The next attacker was up in a tree with a weapon, he rationalized.

Slowing down, J.R. eased up the road to a spot that he could look for an advantage point. He quietly pulled a rifle out of its pouch that was attached to his bike. He could see the sniper standing on a limb about a quarter mile up the trail.

With the vison of a bald eagle, he aimed his assault rifle at the limb, close to the tree. With rapid fire shots, he cut the limb off, and down fell the second cousin! He bounced off the limbs on his way down, and he hit the ground on his back.

"Well, shit," he said, unable to move.

J.R. walked up grinning, and putting that double barrel on the guy's nose, he said, "I hope you are a Christian." Then, as he pulled the hammers back on his gun, J.R. quipped, "If you are, it's time to say a little prayer."

"Wait, wait, I'll tell you anything," said the man as he hacked and coughed, still bothered from the impact of hitting the ground.

"Where's Buster?" J.R. asked. The would-be sniper told him the approximate location of the outlaw. With that, he was left hanging in a second web of ropes.

Buster heard the rifle shots and went into action. He put a stuffed dummy that resembled a man in the driver seat of the wagon. He then started fires on the left and right sides of the trail, down toward where the shots were fired. After a short time, enough time for the fires to spread, he ordered his horses to move forward. Buster, hidden in the bushes, moved along the side of the wagon.

"I'm going to bust that son of an insect's brains out," he said out-loud. He had made himself a large club to do just that. Although he had guns, he wanted to show the law who the true tough guy was and to prove who was the top dog up in these hills. To crack J.R.'s skull was his ultimate goal.

Moving up the trail, J.R. smelled the smoke from the fire. "How stupid — that idiot is going to burn this mountain down," J.R. said to himself.

The smoke threw his senses off, so he parked his bike to finish the job on foot.

Soon, the wagon came into view, and the spider hid behind a huge pine tree. His plan was to get a quick move on his target. By now, the smoke was so thick that Buster's plan was working. J.R. leapt onto the dummy thinking it was Buster. Surprised, he quickly knew this was a trick, but it was too late. Buster caught J.R. on the back of his head with the club. The police helmet took some of the impact, but J.R. was knocked to the ground in a daze. A couple more blows rained down on him as he tried to dodge the club. As the spider venom flowed faster through J.R.'s veins, specifically to his heart and brain, instinct kicked in.

"I've got to strike," he said.

In a flash, he sprang to his feet. With a crushing right hand blow to Buster's mouth, he knocked Buster's teeth everywhere, splitting his lips. The outlaw, Buster Ivans, growled like a grizzly and grabbed J.R. in a bear hug.

"I'm gonna squeeze you in half," he laughed.

"Is that all you got?" asked J.R. He flexed his arms and chest, breaking Buster's grip.

"You're not human, for sure," Buster said, amazed at the tremendous strength J.R. had.

By now the flames had engulfed the whole area, but it didn't faze J.R. The Black Recluse struck with a left hook to the jaw of this huge man. He hit Buster so hard that it knocked him backwards into the flames.

Disoriented and trying to shake off the blow, Buster ran, trying to get away. Big mistake — he darted right back into the middle of the raging firestorm. J.R. could only stand there, rubbing his headache away and hearing the screams that came from the wall of fire. No more moonshine or murders would come from the outlaw Buster Ivans.

After getting the horses to safety, J.R. quickly called the forest rangers to report the fire. He then radioed local law enforcement about the two flies that were caught in spider webs that needed to be jailed.

With that, he disappeared down the trail, anticipating his next adventure.

THE GLOVE

As the days turned into weeks, and weeks into months, J.R.'s life was moving at the speed of light. Working hard in the gym with his police buddies, his strength continued to increase. He was promoted to Sargent under one stipulation — he was not to be taken off motorcycle duties at night. He was, after all, born to be wild.

Somehow, he got involved with helping kids in sports. They loved hanging out with him, and they wanted to be just like him. J.R. realized he was being looked up to as a role model, but meeting that expectation would take some doing on his part.

He was born to be a bad ass, but he would try to live up to what the kids idolized most about him.

It was a good feeling to work with kids, and he was an incredible athlete. It was something that came natural with his inhuman growth.

He wasn't nightclubbing quite as often, nor seeing as many women. His plate was filling up, and there was just not enough time.

His reputation was spreading throughout the south, even to the FBI in Washington D.C. They had been discussing how to use him within the agency. The question was, "How?"

Not only the police, but the bad guys were also quite aware of him. A cartel associate in Atlanta, Georgia had been following J.R. very closely. He had busted a couple of his drug runners, or "mules" as they were called. This guy was known as The Glove. His hand had been chewed off while hunting tigers in India. When he shot a big cat, he had approached the tiger thinking it was dead — wrong! It sprang to life and ripped his hand off and destroyed his eye before his guides were able to kill it. You could also call him Patch because he wore one over his left eye.

The Glove was insane with anger for what J.R. had done with his mules, and he would just as soon kill someone as look at them. He put together a plan to kill the Black Recluse, starting with knowing his hangouts and habits.

He knew of J.R.'s desire for beautiful women, so he placed this drop-dead gorgeous woman in a motel close to the Tennessee mountains, and she registered as being on vacation from Detroit, Michigan. Her job was to go into Knoxville looking for some fun nightlife. The club she chose was where J.R. hung out, but it took two weeks before he showed up.

When she first saw him, she thought, "Oh, what a shame to bring this handsome dude down." Then she muttered to herself, "I'll be the one dead if I don't do my job, though."

It didn't take long before J.R. spotted her on the dance floor. The outfit she was wearing made it hard not to notice her. She had shorts cut short enough to show off her booty, and the cleavage she showed was so amazing it would knock your socks off.

J.R. made his move, but she played it a little "cool," driving him crazy. Eventually, she gave him a dance, and at closing time she said, "Would you like to see the sunrise in the mountains?"

They pulled up to the motel, and she laid a big kiss on J.R.

"You have got to be one of the finest looking women I've had the honor of being in the presence of," he said.

"Can I see all of those bulging muscles that are under that shirt?" she asked.

The trap was working. J.R. had let his guard down because of this woman. This story has been around for a long time, much like Samson and Delilah in the Bible. Now *that* was the ultimate superhero of all time, and he was a real human. The biblical story tells of how he took on an army of one thousand soldiers with just the jawbone of an ass. He crushed them all, not to mention he grabbed a lion by the mouth and ripped it apart. Now that was "BAD." But anyway, back to J.R.

Kelly Anne poured J.R. a tall glass of wine. With her back to him, she dropped in three powerful sedatives and stirred them quietly. After pouring herself some, she handed J.R. the concoction.

"Here's to a wonderful night with a handsome man," she told him.

With that, they make a toast and downed the drinks. She played her role like a seasoned Hollywood actress. After a couple of romantic hugs and kisses, J.R. started feeling woozy. The drugs were doing their job. He dropped to one knee while holding onto a chair, and looking into her eyes, he knew instantly what was happening.

After Kelly Anne smiled, she said, "Sweet dreams, my fine spider-man." Then, she picked up the phone and called the hitman who was waiting outside in a car.

J.R. knew he had been drugged, so he reached way down in his "gorilla bag" to find some venom to inject so that he could pump some more blood to his brain in order to overtake the drugs. After what would have taken down ten men, J.R. was holding on surprisingly well and even pulled himself into a chair.

Kelly Anne looked at him, and if looks could kill, she would have been a bag full of refried beans. His piercing, dark eyes were burning a hole right through her.

As the hitman came in, she screamed, "Shoot quickly and let's get the flying shit out of here. I don't know if those drugs are going to keep him down."

J.R. was almost on his feet and was reaching for his pistol when the scar-faced hitman fired two shots into his chest, and with that, the two killers disappeared into the dark.

Because of the loud commotion, the motel manager came running to see what in the Lord's creation was going on. He found J.R. laying on his back with blood pouring out of his chest and back.

"This ain't good," the manager said. After calling an ambulance and then the cops, he did what he could to try and stop the bleeding with towels.

The cops arrived first and started C.P.R. until the paramedics could get there. They checked J.R.'s wallet and soon discovered that this was the one and only Black Recluse they had been hearing so much about. As the news hit the airways, the FBI scrambled to meet at the hospital where the ambulance was taking J.R. He was hanging on to life like a wounded spider in its web.

Paramedics were leaving no machine or medication out to help J.R. survive. One bullet pierced a lung, and the other busted his breastbone, which barely missed his heart.

"How can this man still be breathing? He should be dead," they said.

The ambulance reached the local hospital where a group of doctors were ready to try and save J.R. Straight into the operating room they went where each specialized doctor took their turn in trying to patch J.R. up.

One bullet was removed, but the other had gone straight through his body. All night and most of the next day, they worked frantically to stabilize him.

One thing they didn't know — J.R. was not exactly human. His chances of survival were better than anyone's.

Once the doctors in charge gave the head of the Tennessee Division of the FBI permission to talk in private with J.R., a complex decision had already been made.

As the FBI chief entered the dim hospital room, he saw a bandaged person lying in a bed with IVs and machines hooked into his body. He could tell J.R. was terribly weak from his wounds.

He slowly walked over to J.R. and said, "Hang in there, man, we need you." J.R.'s steel eyes glared up at him, and the stranger thought, "I'd better introduce myself."

"Mr. Dawkins, my name is Lester Johnson, and I'm head of the FBI here in Tennessee," he said.

A slightly puzzled look came over J.R.'s face. It had been a while since anyone had addressed him as Mr. Dawkins.

Then Lester said, "J.R. we've been following you for quite a while, ever since you joined the police force. I think I have an offer you can't refuse. I don't know how you have such superior instincts and strength, but don't think it's been going unnoticed by people in higher places."

He explained how he knew all about his background, all the way back to the time he was four years old and was bitten multiple times by a poisonous spider.

"Why are you so intrigued by the black recluse spider?" Lester asked. J.R. just gave him that piercing stare again, not saying anything.

Mr. Johnson rambled on making small talk for a while, knowing he had to win J.R.'s trust if he was going to get any answers.

After talking for some time, J.R. finally said, "Just what do you want from me?"

With that opening, Lester said, "Let me introduce you to a top secret plan we have to offer — only you and a select few will even know the truth about it."

J.R. sensed something big was about to happen in his life, and that old "excitement" he was born with kicked in.

Lester said, "Here's the plan. You didn't survive the attack, and you're officially dead. The hospital administrator will be sworn to secrecy, then we will have you 'cremated' with a big memorial with family and friends to make it believable." He had his fingers crossed hoping J.R. would agree.

"That would be hard to live with. All my family and friends thinking I'm dead," J.R. said with a tear in his eye.

"Tell you what — if I talk with your mom and dad, feel them out, and decide they can be trusted, will you do it?" Lester bargained.

J.R. thought for a while, then said, "Maybe, but what kind of plans do you have for me if I do decide to play dead?"

"We will make you a special suit and motorcycle that would be so futuristically designed that no criminal could compete against you. Your cycle will have a machine gun and rocket launchers on board. The suit and helmet will be bulletproof, then you will go into the most rigorous training you could never even imagine. Extreme weightlifting, karate, knife throwing, etc.," Lester excitingly explained.

"How about showing me some credentials," J.R. blurted out.

"No problem, Mr. Dawkins. Should have done that sooner. I like your attitude," Lester said.

With that taken care of, they settled into more conversation. The more Lester talked, the more J.R. wanted to hear. His patented grin flashed, and he said, "Go on, I'm listening."

"Your suit and motorcycle will glow in the dark with you controlling it. In other words, we want you to 'come back' as a ghost. That will scare the shit out of everyone! You have been selected by the FBI to be a secret weapon for us. Criminals will be caught off guard, and we could use something new to help us fight the war on crime," Lester said, out of breath.

"In all my crazy and wild dreams, I never thought something this thrilling and mysterious would come my way," J.R. laughed, with a pain shooting through his chest.

After discussing more details about the proposal, J.R. said, "I tell you what — if you'll do something for me, I might just take you up on this scheme."

"Anything, what do you want me to do?" Lester asked.

"I'm going to tell you something that only a few people know," J.R. whispered.

Excitedly, Lester leaned a little closer and said, "By all means, what can I do for you?"

Slowly, J.R. explained to him what happened when he was bitten by the black recluse spider when he was young, how good it made him feel, and how addicted he had become to the venom.

"So that's your secret, how you are so unordinary compared to other people," Chief Lester said, not really understanding how something that kills could do that for someone.

"Go to my apartment, look in the fridge — there's a hidden panel. Push it over, then up. You will find some vials of venom I've collected. Get them to me as soon as possible. It will help me survive these wounds better than whatever this stuff is that they're pumping into me," J.R. hurriedly explained.

"I'll personally go. My agents will proceed with everything to make this happen, and I hope you're right. You have got to survive this. Does this mean we have a deal?" Lester asked.

"Yeah," J.R. blurted out. With that one word, the final metamorphoses of the "Black Recluse" began!

J.R. was quietly moved into a room that adjoined the morgue. It took two weeks to upgrade him from the critical stage he had been in. The venom undoubtedly saved his life. The small group that knew the truth about the death of J.R. was sworn to secrecy, and his death was announced to the world. Their plan was working.

Supposedly, J.R. was cremated, and his ashes were sprinkled at one of his favorite places in Kantrell Crossing. The ashes were nothing but corn meal, but nobody could tell the difference.

Lester Johnson was a bad customer in his own right. He trained recruits in martial arts, and his muscles and bones were as tough as rawhide. He couldn't wait to get J.R. trained and increase his strength even more. Lester was sixty-two with tons of experience and know-how. He had top scientists study the spider venom to find why it worked in J.R.

Even though he had been experimenting with this phenomenon for a long time, J.R. couldn't help the scientists. They came up with no answers; they were completely blank. What they did discover was a way to enhance the venom to ten times its normal potency. By making it more concentrated, it worked even better when J.R. injected it. He was growing into someone even more inhuman. The FBI loved it, and man, did Lester have plans for him!

After three months of training, it was time to introduce J.R. to his police uniform and motorcycle. They were awesome, even more so than J.R. could imagine. The glow of the uniform that could only be regulated by him made the ghost effect eerie to see. The dark of night was soon to be ignited into a hellish light! Inside his suit was a microphone, close to his throat with a micro speaker that amplified his voice. This made him sound like he was speaking from the grave.

Everything he wore was bulletproof, designed with space- age technology. When he laid eyes on his modified motorcycle, all J.R. could mutter was, "Have mercy!" Two hundred miles an hour with special shocks that let him go airborne and come down smooth as silk. The bike was all black with that black recluse spider on the windshield. It even had fiery red eyes that penetrated the darkness. They would make you crap on yourself.

A machine gun over the front fender and four rocket launchers made the Black Recluse loaded for bear. This ideal look was to establish a ghost that returned to earth.

A meeting was held at the Nashville FBI headquarters. "It's time that our top-secret weapon is unleashed," Lester said. "First, from now on in all documented communication, I will be referred to as L.J., and J.R. will be B.R.," the chief explained. This was just to cover their tracks on paper since technically J.R. was dead.

"Okay, but I'm telling you, I have a score to settle with one foxy lady and a glove," B.R. demanded.

"We have to do this right. Remember, you will only appear from the grave at night. Let's make that on a full moon night," the chief snickered.

Working with the FBI in Georgia, L.J. researched all the information he could get on The Glove. He knew B.R. would be on his own in the streets of Atlanta because he was returning from the grave, and not even everyone in the department knew the plan.

A popular section of the city was called Underground Atlanta or the Old City. Opened in the 1960s, it was a city beneath the main city. There was a shopping and entertainment district in the Five Points area of Underground Atlanta. It was three levels deep and a very popular part of town.

L.J.'s research led him to a theory that there may be a fourth level which had been overlooked.

Word on the street told him The Glove was spotted quite a few times going in and out of the Old City.

"This has got to be where The Glove operates," L.J. said to his agents.

They knew of his involvement with drugs, but what else was he into? His lifestyle showed that he was raking in a ton of cash.

After further investigation, the FBI discovered a large complex down on this fourth level. This info was gained by an undercover agent. The Glove had an elaborate operation set up there that consisted of drugs, prostitutes, gambling, and even a restaurant with a food menu second to none. Things like African lion chops, South American wild antelope steaks, Sockeye salmon from Alaska, and so many other illegal foods were on the menu. To become a member of this plush hideaway, you had to be wealthy with a background check for loyalty. It was operated with precision as a top-secret sin nest, complete with bedrooms people could stay in for as long as they liked. The cost averaged around five thousand dollars a night per person, and it was always full.

Two blocks up on the main street was a tanning and massage parlor. The people that ran it were employed by The Glove. This was the secret entry way down to the fourth level complex. There was a hidden stairwell and door that led to the sin nest, but this couldn't be seen by normal people as they came in or out of the shop. It was very well hidden.

The Glove very seldom left the complex, but why would he with anything he wanted at his disposal?

A room in a hotel was reserved by the FBI to watch the movements in Underground Atlanta. This was achieved by an agent being disguised as a businessman from Chicago. Surveillance was on, 24/7, until they could make calculated plans.

The agency discovered that The Glove's mother was in a nursing home with dementia. On the same night every week, he would go visit her, even though she didn't recognize him.

The agents observed that The Glove left the main Old City entrance in a limousine with tinted windows on Tuesday nights at seven o'clock. They assumed the windows were bulletproof and that the car was full of bodyguard cronies. Would this pose a serious problem for B.R., having to bring all those gangsters down while convincing everyone he was something of a "ghost?"

B.R. was asked this question during his briefing about the setup.

He simply gave that grin and said, "Piece of cake." He wasn't afraid of anything or any situation. "I'm loving it! Besides, I owe that bastard, and I'm gonna make him pay up," B.R. said, laughing.

"Float like a butterfly, sting like a bee. That phrase should have been said about me," J.R. said.

Plans were made, and the whole operation was moved into hiding in Atlanta. The FBI would be all around, but out of sight. Only B.R. would be seen.

Monday night, B.R. was pacing the floor. He was so hyped up and ready to ride into the darkness of night again that he couldn't sit still. He was so ready to take his rage out through this act of revenge on the pair that almost brought him down.

B.R. had the vengeful mentality, "I'll get you back!"

L.J. ordered a sedative to attempt to settle B.R. down so that he would be at the top of his game. With a good day's sleep, the hours ticked closer to "roll time."

B.R. looked at L.J. and said, "I don't know why you're so fussy — I'm the meanest son of a bitch in Atlanta."

All L.J. could do was laugh, knowing that he was right.

The suit was on, the motorcycle was loaded, and the sun was going down. As B.R. rolled out of the dark, hidden door, all the lights on the bike were off. His vision was as sharp as a falcon, even in the darkness, which gave him an advantage over the bad guys. Spider venom was flowing rampant through his veins, and B.R. was reacting like the spider he was named for as he closed in on his prey.

The limo pulled out, right on schedule, and B.R. followed, keeping his distance. He wanted to get out of the heavy traffic and attack in a more secluded part of town, like where the nursing home was located. To do this, B.R. had to ride on sidewalks and alleyways to not be spotted by innocent people. He and his bike were like one welded together machine — all black and wicked.

As traffic thinned out, B.R. pulled up close to the limo and flipped on his eerie lights so that they would shine into the car's rearview mirror. The driver freaked, so much so that he almost ran off the road. Everyone turned and saw B.R. with his long, blood red scarf glowing. They pulled their weapons out to engage this "thing" that was on their bumper.

"I don't know what it is, but I'm going to make it history," said one of the bodyguards.

Hitting the window buttons on both sides, the bodyguards leaned out and the guns started firing back toward B.R. That was when the "ghost" showed proof that he had returned from the grave. The motorcycle that was specially built for B.R. went into action.

A couple of cars that were parked on the side of the road were among the first to help the Black Recluse fly through the air. As he aimed for the back of the first parked car, B.R. pulled back on the handlebars to pop a wheelie, and he went up and over the two cars. This maneuver was accomplished without putting a scratch on either car. The special shocks absorbed the lift and impact to the vehicles and the ground when he finally did touch ground. B.R. "flew" through the air, much like a spider swinging on its silk. If only Evil Knievel had venom and a kick-ass motorcycle!

When the thugs saw this flying mystery in the air, they were flabbergasted. "What in hell's name are we dealing with?" one asked.

B.R. pulled his pistol out and fired a shot at the limo's window just to see if it was bulletproof. The assumption was correct because the bullet bounced off. Guns were blazing from the car, but B.R. was zigzagging making it harder to hit him. If he did get shot, though, his body armor would protect him.

Angrily, B.R. geared down and pulled his trusty shotgun. One barrel took out one tire, and the other barrel took down the next. Traveling at a high speed, the limo driver lost control and flipped over and over, slamming into a culvert upside down. The driver and front seat rider were thrown against the windshield and killed on impact. They weren't really bright; neither of them were wearing a seatbelt.

As B.R. rolled to a stop, he saw a person with long hair crawl out the middle window.

"Well, well, my old flame. The foxy lady," he said to her. He noticed The Glove was lying on the road and not moving, but he also saw a tommy gun lying beside him.

Two other bodyguards crawled out, dazed, but with guns in hand. Foxy lady fired a shot that struck B.R. square in the gut, but all she saw and heard was the "ghost" laughing a creepy laugh.

She just stared and said, "Who are you?"

B.R. answered in that eerie voice and told her, "I'm the Black Recluse, returned from the grave!"

Thinking the bullet went through his body, she turned and tried to limp off.

The other two aimed to shoot but saw nothing. B.R. had his ghost lights turned off, and the next thing the shooters knew, he was behind them. Fast as lightning, B.R. whacked one, then the other right across the face with his sawed-off shotgun, leaving them unconscious.

Running Foxy Lady down was easy. He used a smooth, silk-like rope and quickly tied her up like a bug in a web.

Going back to The Glove, B.R. saw this leader of the pack getting his bearings and hobbling upright. The Black Recluse turned his lights back on so The Glove could see him, and he said, "Hold on punk, I'm going to give you a fighting chance, which is more than I got."

The Glove said, "I thought you were dead?"

B.R. laughed and said, "I am, and you are, too, either way you go."

The Glove, with gun in hand, angrily moved his trigger finger to fire. Faster than the gunslinger Clint Eastwood, B.R. drew his shotgun from the holster and, with both barrels, literally cut this gangster in half. The Spider was quick as a "blink," and he was the last thing The Glove ever saw.

After blowing the smoke from his shotgun and reloading, he radioed L.J. and said, "What's next?"

FOXY LADY

The FBI and police arrived on the scene, but found only two unconscious men along with what was left of the Glove. The silk rope hanging from the tree limbs was torn and empty. Foxy Lady had cut herself loose with a small knife she had hidden in her panties just as the Black Recluse rode off. She hobbled over to the next street, and with her clothes torn and covered in blood, she flagged a car to a screeching stop. Crying, she told the driver that she had been attacked and asked to be taken to a hospital. So the woman told her she would take her where she wanted to go.

As she climbed into the back seat, Foxy said, "Oh, thank you so much," while she was pulling a short piece of piano wire from inside her bra.

Swiftly, she wrapped it around the woman's neck and leaned back, applying so much pressure on the wire that the driver could hardly breath.

"I'll kill you if you don't stop," Foxy said. The woman slammed on the breaks in panic and stopped the car. When the car came to a halt, Foxy twisted the wire and pulled it deep into the woman's neck, cutting her jugular. With no air and squirting blood, the poor woman fell over dead.

Foxy pulled her out of the car and raced off into the night. When another car came down the road, the driver saw the woman in the street and drove to a pay phone to call the police. The police arrived quickly, thinking this may have been connected to what had just happened with The Glove just a few blocks away. As luck would have it, Foxy didn't notice that the woman had her purse wrapped around her arm when she was pushed out of the car. The cops found her driver's license and insurance registration, and they quickly identified the woman and the car. An all points alarm hit the airways, and B.R. heard it while still on his Harley. After doing a smoking U-turn and burning rubber for a block long, he picked up the chase.

It only took a couple of minutes for a patrolman to spot the stolen vehicle as it went roaring by. B.R. heard the call and the spider venom hit overdrive. With ghost lights off and motoring near 150 mph, he was literally "flying." Now, Foxy had hit Highway 41 going south toward Macon, Georgia, and the Chevy she was driving was maxed out with the pedal to the metal. Thinking she had pulled the escape off, Foxy breathed a sigh of relief and smiled.

"I've kicked his ass again," she said out loud. But no, no, Foxy — the super instincts of the Black Recluse were like a radar zeroing in!

Running upwards of 200 mph, the Recluse flipped on his ghost lights and had the angry Harley Davidson engine "screaming." Just as B.R. had the Chevy in his sights, a lone state trooper up ahead had pulled his squad car sideways on the highway, blocking the road. Standing in the middle of the road behind the driver's door, he saw Foxy coming straight at him, not letting up on the gas. As she got close enough for the trooper to see, he put both hands on his gun and pointed it straight at her face. He closed one eye, squeezed the trigger, and "splat" — the bullet shattered the windshield and hit her dead-center, right between the eyes. The policeman dove out of the way just in the nick of time. The Chevy hit the patrol car at full speed which sent a huge fireball into the sky.

B.R. pulled up, and in that ghostly voice said, "Where in hell did you learn to shoot like that?" Before the state trooper could answer, the Black Recluse was gone.

BACK TO NASHVILLE

L.J. had decided to bench B.R. awhile and, instead, placed him in the office to use his computer-like brain on difficult FBI projects. He would study a case, make calculated deductions, and decide which direction the agency should take. Doing this type of work was time consuming, and it kept B.R. tied up for quite a while. This was not what he liked to do, but he respected the agency's confidence in him. This was, after all, very critical work on very complicated crimes around the world.

One case he really had to dig into was pink-colored cocaine that came out of Peru. It was treasured by big-shot high rollers worldwide. It was purer and more potent; it was considered to be the rich man's coke which made it very expensive. Because of the large profits that were made from this cocaine, the producers were getting more aggressive and dangerous. They were distributing it all over the world from one of the Peruvian jungles by mules, trucks, planes, and even small submarines. It was carried out every way that could be imagined.

The plan to shut down this crippling drug was high on the law enforcements to-do list. B.R.'s job was to find the best way to move on the compound hidden in the jungles of Colombia and Peru. Native medicine men and witch doctors were the ones who knew the secret of cooking the coca leaves and making the cocaine, but no one, except the ones who cooked this batch, knew why this particular powder had the pink tint. Was it the technique, or was it just the Peruvian coca plant? These were some of the questions B.R. was assigned to figure out.

CHANGES

As B.R. continued to hash through the FBI's pending cases and ponder further on the logistics of the pink cocaine, Chief L.J. hurriedly entered the room and said, "Gonna have to put this desk stuff on hold for a while. You can come back to it, but something really important has come up. I know how bad you want back on your steel horse, so guess what? You're getting your wish and pronto."

B.R. stated excitedly, "Oh really! This must be bad to take me off such important cases." He could tell something was really going down by the look in L.J.'s eyes.

"We have just had a police massacre happen at a bank robbery gone wrong," replied L.J.

"Tell me what you know," demanded B.R.

Starting from the beginning of what he had found out,

L.J. explained how this all came about. He told a story of a renegade biker that had a split personality affliction. A big and mean type of guy with a burning desire to create the most notorious and bad ass biker club in America. He was sick and tired of hearing about how tough all the other clubs were, so he began recruiting bikers that were interested in his idea and then put them through a very physical course to see if they were man enough to be one of his new gang members. He made them do things that showed how well they could ride and handle their motorcycle, fight, and shoot their gun. If they passed his course, they were officially a member of Satan's Saints, the meanest biker brigade in the U.S.A.

They financed their evil club by dealing drugs and pimping out biker prostitutes. A kilo of cocaine could manufacture a tremendous amount of dough, and they were moving one a week.

Big Bubba was the ringleader, and he continued to recruit biker gang members. His goal was to live a more lavish lifestyle than all the other biker gangs, and he wanted to be known as the meanest gang. In order to achieve this, they needed more money. They needed to become the pace-setter for all bike gangs, current and future. Big Bubba decided to start robbing banks. They would be feared by everyone, including the police. The bikers of the S.S. club were drinking, using drugs, and raising hell, which gave them the image they strived to create.

BANK ROBBERS

As Big Bubba laid out his robbery plan, he purchased a map of the United States. As he looked around the adjoining states of Illinois, he found a small town in South Dakota that was in a lightly populated area. Rapid City, South Dakota was located directly north of the Badlands National Park and provided access to Highway 240, Badlands Loop Road.

The Lakota Sioux Indians were the first to call this place "Mako Sica" or "Land Bad." Extreme temperatures, lack of water, and the exposed rugged terrain led to this name. In the early 1900s, French Canadian fur trappers called it "Les Mauvais Terres Pour Traverse" or "badlands to travel through."

The more Big Bubba studied the area, the more intrigued he became with this desolate part of the world, and he learned quite a bit to his liking. Visiting the Badlands of South Dakota was like stepping into a moonscape on earth.

The Badlands offer a stunning example of geological variety — jagged cliffs, deep canyons, and shape buttes formed by relentless forces of nature. There are park trails, limitless back country, hiking, backpacking, and camping. To Big Bubba this was a perfect location to hide out in after a bank hit.

Perched high on the edge of sunburned cliffs, the city of Wall got its name from the rugged ramparts that form the north rim of South Dakota's Badlands. It is a "gateway" community to Badlands National Park. Wall boasts of eleven motels, seven restaurants, museums, campgrounds, auto services, a medical clinic, and a golf course.

"This will be like taking candy from a baby," Bubba determined.

THE PLAN

After gathering all the information he could on this area in South Dakota, Big Bubba determined this would be a great place to start a reign of bank robberies. This place was sparsely populated, and there would not be many police officers on duty. It was isolated, and there was all of those barren Badlands to hide out in, just in case they need to disappear.

The next day, Bubba began putting the "pros" of hitting the Badlands down on paper. He had decided there were no "cons" to the decision. The only problem he saw was how to fit in as a tourist. With this question circulating in his head, he remembered reading about the little town of Wall, South Dakota. All of the motels to stay in made it seem possible that he could do two weeks in one, two weeks in another, and so on. Bubba grinned as he thought of how many banks could be hit in six weeks, all while staying in the Wall motels.

"This could be easier than I ever dreamed it to be," he told himself.

He called a meeting of all the gang members, and told them flat out, "We are going to rob some banks and live like kings!"

He could hear some low grumbling coming from a few of his counterparts. "If anyone is not up for it, don't let the door hit your ass as you leave, and if you breathe a word of what we are doing, I will cut your tongue out," Big Bubba shouted.

Everyone was quiet for a while until one outspoken biker said, "Well, what's your plan? We're wasting time."

With that, everyone said they were in, and Bubba explained his plan, starting with Wall. He did ask if anyone had suggestions on how to improve on his theory. They all made suggestions, and Bubba listened intently. At the end, though, Big Bubba's alter-ego came out and he said, "If y'all are gonna disagree with my mastery, I'll blow your head off."

This is what made him so dangerous. When it was just him, his mind would wander, but when his split personality presented itself to others, things got violent.

After they all had their say, they came up with this adapted plan. Only eight people would rent motel rooms in Wall during the first two weeks. The rest of the gang would stay in Chicago to keep the local operations going. When the two weeks were up, seven members would switch places. They could run this system for quite a while since the club had grown to thirty-eight members so far.

They guessed that they could hit four banks during each two week stay. Big Bubba would coordinate the robberies at the motel but would not participate in the robbery itself. He alone would deliver the money back to Chicago since he didn't trust anyone.

Most of the bikers were decent mechanics, so they purchased an old, broken down Ford truck that would blend in. Taking the motor and transmission out, they replaced them with a Hemi engine, transmission, super charger, and racing gear all out of a Dodge. They installed low-noise mufflers to disguise the powerful sound coming from the motor. A heavy- duty, straight shift transmission was also locked into place, and a low sheen black paint job made it the perfect getaway ride to hit a bank. With a small back seat, four bikers could fit inside the cab, but it was tight. The other three would be waiting at the outskirts of town on their bikes posing as tourists. If anything went "south," they were there for support. Once a bank was robbed, they would take the truck out into the Badlands, and with a generator and spray paint gun, presto, the truck was painted a different color. By changing the license plate each time, no one could trace the getaway vehicle. Big Bubba could visualize himself on the French Riviera gazing at the hundreds of topless French beauties on the beach and with a slop bucket full of money to spend!

After a week of preparation, everything was a go. The seven bikers and Bubba traveled to Wall with the motorcycles and truck. Wearing business-type clothes instead of their normal leathers, they checked into a motel and left the truck at a camping resort, not to be used until robbery time. They chose a bank in Rapid City, which was about fifty-six miles away and seemed perfect for their first hit. The bikers arrived on a Saturday, making Monday the right time to strike. Their goal was two banks a week. Sunday night, everything was laid out at the motel. Overalls, hats, masks, and fake glasses were all part of their disguises.

HAMMER TIME

Early Monday morning, the gang members were packing everything up to make the hour drive to Rapid City. All the bikers except those in the truck rode their spit-shined Harley Hog's. They were all different styles and colors which made them a sight to behold, but if someone touched one, they would cut their hands off.

Around eight o'clock, they arrived in Rapid City, as they wanted to strike right after opening time at nine. The bank employees would be preparing for the day and foot traffic would be low. The truck was parked across the street, and the three bikers were about half a mile away pretending to be tourists looking for leather shop garments. They stayed where they could see the bank and what was going on, though.

One of the members in the truck wore a Frank Sinatra style hat, a pair of fake eyeglasses, and long sideburns. He took out a partial plate from his mouth which left two empty spaces in his mouth. Dressed in a Hawaiian shirt and slacks, he casually walked into the bank along with two other customers. As he walked up to a bank teller, he handed her a blank check and asked if she could cash it? When the teller looked own at the check, she read BANK ROBBERY. He slowly pointed a gun straight at her head, and said, "Do not make a sound."

Slowly, she looked up and saw the other three men inside the front door wearing overalls and pointing guns at other employees around the bank. One robber yelled, "On the floor, or I will kill all of you!"

The robber that handed the teller the blank check pulled a large bag from his deep pocket and said, "Every last dollar from the money safe, and you might live to see the evening sunset. I understand it is gorgeous here in South Dakota."

He followed her to the safe as she started shaking from head to toe. She opened the door and proceeded to fill the bag with all the money in the safe as he told her, "Just the large bills, no one dollars, please."

She was thinking, "They are going kill me once they have what they want."

She started sobbing and begging him not to shoot her. "I have three small children and they need me — please!" she cried.

The robbers knew killing someone would make it a lot harder to get away with robbing the other banks, but they didn't want the victims to know that.

With all the money inside of the bag, they all headed for the door, reminding everyone in the building that if anyone did anything stupid, they would hunt down their families and massacre them all. The customers lying on the floor had pissed all over the place and were praying out loud.

The four jumped into the truck, revved the Hemi, and were off to meet the three members who had kept their distance so no one would suspect them as being part of the robbery. Away they went into the Badlands, disappearing until twilight set in. By then, they would have repainted the truck and headed back into Wall.

Big Bubba counted the stash, and with a big sinister laugh and tears in his eyes from greed, he said, "742,000 dollars isn't bad for a day's worth of work."

They were all so excited that they hooped and hollered and danced with one another like school kids.

"I'm going to get me a suite in Las Vegas with five prostitutes," one biker said, giddily.

Bubba left in a hurry to take the haul to Chicago so that it could be distributed among the rest of the gang. Right before he left, though, he prepped the current group of gang members on the next robbery, which would take place the following Thursday in Deadwood, South Dakota.

While Bubba was gone, the bikers back in Walls cranked up their Harleys and went on a scenic cruise through parts of the Black Hills all the way to Mount Rushmore National Memorial. They were to lay low for a while to keep from creating any suspicion. Satan's Saints may have been viciously mean, but they were not stupid.

Deadwood was a city known for its gold rush history. Mount Moriah Cemetery held the graves of Wild West figures like Wild Bill Hickok and Calamity Jane. Exhibits at the Adams Museum included a huge gold nugget and a plesiosaur dinosaur fossil, and the historic Adams House, built in 1892, was a Victorian mansion that had all of its original features. South of town, the George S. Mickelson Trail snaked through the Black Hills National Forest. This was a trail that this group of bikers actually enjoyed. That was saying a lot for a bunch of outlaws!

The motorcycle riding band of bank robbers, while studying Deadwood, discovered all the history about the place, and one commented, "I wish Wild Bill was still alive because I'd love to see how fast he actually was on his draw. I bet I could take him," he said braggingly.

Another member mentioned hitting the museum for the huge, priceless gold nugget.

They all laughed at him and said, "You couldn't even carry it."

He shot them all a bird.

Big Bubba returned, though, and they carried on making plans for the upcoming bank robbery on that Thursday. Everything was laid out pretty much the same as the first robbery except the men swapped roles. The ones in the bank were now on motorcycles and vice versa. The robbery happened much like the first one, except the money haul was close to a million dollars this time. They had literally cleaned out every large bill this bank had. Success smelled so sweet to Big Bubba, and his greed let his mind wander to the empire he was going to build and rule. The wealthiest and most feared biker gang of all time was running on cruise control.

THEN CAME MORTAL SIN

Two more banks were hit with different sets of bikers. Things were really beginning to heat up with law enforcement, as they had determined that the heists were serial robberies that involved the same group of people. It was time for Big Bubba to change his strategy to throw the law dogs off their scent. So, he backed off for a while and did some more geographical evaluations, but his split personality affliction changed his thought process in the middle of all this. He got extremely angry, thinking, "Why doesn't any good-looking, movie star actress type want to shack up with me?" The big, homely looking ox was in tears!

Eventually, he came up with Wisconsin being the next target. There would be so much cash for them all to burn. Bubba's thought process changed to how they could rob an armored truck, making one huge money haul so that they could retire from robberies and cruise the world on their bikes as the most success-ful biker club, enjoying the easy life and raising hell.

Keeping that idea in the back of his mind, he de-cided to move on to the small city of Waukesha, Wis-consin. It is part of the Milwaukee metropolitan area with a population of around seventy thousand. Mil-waukee just happened to be home to the famous Har-ley Davidson Motorcycle plant that made the now fa-mous Black Recluse's bike of choice, and Waukesha was only one hundred miles from Chicago.

Bubba figured they could use the same robbery method as before because of its success back in South Dakota. He picked a bank and a motel for this next heist, and since the city was bigger, Bubba figured there would be a lot more money to haul off.

The plan was laid out, and the seven Saints blew into Waukesha on a late Friday night, creating the same timing to strike on Monday morning. They spent the weekend in Milwaukee, hanging out in night clubs where the bands were pumping out the sound of the times — rock and roll music.

Motown, Beatles, James Brown, and Elvis were some of the selections that were popular in this major city in Wisconsin.

Sunday night found the bikers laying around the motel and contemplating the plan for the next morning. Everything was much on schedule, and as the last cigarette was smoked, the lights went out and a restless sleep was attempted.

Early Monday morning, the bikers prepared for their execution of the robbery with the anticipation of bringing home a huge duffle bag full of green. When the first robber walked through the door, handed the teller the slip, and demanded the cash, a male teller secretly stepped on an alarm button installed on the floor. That button immediately signaled the precinct just a few blocks away. This bank was much more advanced than the small ones in South Dakota they had hit, as the robbers soon found out. While the money was being placed in the bag, the streets outside were swarming with cops. The biker sitting in the truck across the street slid down and pulled a Thompson machine gun out from under the seat. He laid in waiting for just the right moment.

All the commotion outside alarmed the three bikers inside, so they grabbed the customers lying on the floor as hostages and forgot all about the money bag. Escape was the main goal at this moment, no matter what it took.

As all the cops gathered at the front door, the robber in the truck sprang into action He had gone completely unnoticed by the cops. He took aim and began blasting away, taking one cop down after another. The two on motorcycles came roaring down the street to assist, shooting the unsuspecting policemen with deadly accuracy. The surprise response by the gang resulted in a crossfire of biker bullets.

With the cops trying to take cover, the three inside darted out with the hostages, got to the truck, and fled town with that hemi engine burning half the rubber off the back tires. Big Bubba had made emergency plans before even the first heist, which was to split up and go in different directions, then circle and meet at an isolated spot. They would quickly repaint the truck and hide out until dark. Then they would take different roads back to Chicago. This plan worked, and all the bikers had survived and were safe — for now!

It was a different story for the police precinct in Waukesha, Wisconsin. Four policemen were dead and seven more were injured, some being in critical condition. The local hospital was slammed. A call had gone out for a very rare blood type — AB — for one of the injured. It was a female officer, and she was clinging to life because she had lost so much blood. Someone finally responded, but it was too late. She didn't make it, and now the death toll was up to five.

It was determined that whoever these robbers were at Waukesha, it was the same people that had robbed the banks in South Dakota. This made the case a federal problem now.

F.B.I. INTERVENTION

After L.J. finished telling the story, he ordered B.R. to pack everything he needed because it was now on the FBI to bring this problem to a halt and as soon as possible. All FBI agencies knew of B.R.'s reputation, and his security clearance could put him anywhere in the world. Everyone had heard he was from the grave, but all of the agents kept their beliefs to themselves. They were just glad that he was on their side.

L.J. didn't know exactly what the case file on his desk held, but now it was their job to fit all of the unanswered pieces together. Chicago was the center point of both locations, and the chief figured that B.R., with those sixth senses, could put the rest together. He knew that whatever the Recluse faced, he could handle it. Killing cops made you an "in-the-crosshairs" criminal.

B.R.'s plan was to move into Chicago with top secret clearance. He hand-picked the agents to go with him. One was Bob Jarvis, a Mexican American with a Cheech and Chong personality that B.R. liked. They were all going in undercover. Whenever he got an idea of what was going on, he needed them to help create an offensive strategy and serve as backup.

Just as they had done in Atlanta with The Glove, they set up operation in a deserted warehouse next to Lake Michigan. It was FBI sealed and protected. B.R. got all the information that was on file about the robberies in South Dakota and Wisconsin, and on a large table, he laid it all out and began his uncanny, spider-like calculations. After living with it for a couple of days, the pattern started to come into view.

Harley Davidson motorcycles had to be the connecting clue. They were always present in the police reports. Question was, who used those machines and were evil enough to gun down police officers? It didn't take a rocket scientist to figure that out — a biker gang! Since there are a lot of biker gangs, but not a lot of cop killers, B.R. had to figure out what motorcycle clubs could be both.

B.R. told Bob to get hold of a Japanese bike as soon as possible. He told his other agents to spread out across Chicago and find out where the roughest of the rough bikers hung out. After putting on the right clothes and wearing a full-face motorcycle shield to disguise himself, B.R. rode the Japanese bike around Chicago, watching for groups on Harley's. He found most of the biker hangouts and got laughed at when he pulled into one, which was his plan: a Japanese bike in a parking lot of Harleys!

After about a week, one of the agents, who was pretending that he wanted to become a rider with a club, ran into an alcoholic biker who would blab about anything. All it took was some scotch whiskey, and he would answer whatever was asked. Through him, the agent found out about the notorious Satan's Saints and about their growing reputation of being the most bad ass biker club in the area. This raised a red flag, and he contacted Jarvis immediately.

Without a doubt, B.R. knew this was the gang they had been looking for. It was in his DNA. Getting back with the agent that found the information, B.R. told him, "Buy the man a bottle of Cutty Sark, and find out all he knows about Satan's Saints. I'll personally send Chief L.J. a bill for that scotch."

The subject, in a drunken stupor, explained to the agent about Big Bubba's recruitment of members on the back streets of Chicago. He also said that he knew where to reach Bubba, or, maybe he didn't. The alcohol had burned some of his brain cells.

B.R. decided that the place the alcoholic had mentioned could possibly be the right place to find Big Bubba. Just like Kid Shelleen in the 1965 movie Cat Ballou, B.R. unveiled his Black Recluse outfit, started the engine on his custom Harley, and jetted into the dark Chicago night. With his lights off, he traveled down back streets and alleyways to the out-skirts of town. He found a well-built log barn that housed the Satan's Saints. He saw a tower and guard in front of a chain link fence. It was the kind of stuff found at a prison. It even had the razor wire on top.

As the lookout was peering toward the road, he heard a rattle from down below in the bushes. Not being able to see what made the sound, he got down and walked over to where the noise came from with his pistols cocked.

"Who in hell's name is there," the guard de-manded.

He felt a light touch on his shoulder, and as he quickly turned, a double barreled, pistol gripped shot-gun landed squarely across his nose. He was knocked senseless, but somehow, as he was hit, the trigger was pulled on one of the guns. With a loud BOOM echoing through the distance, B.R. knew whoever was inside would be coming out soon.

With two long strides the B.R. was back on his iron horse with his ghost lights glowing. He blew open the gate, headed toward the barn entrance, and with another rocket blew the door apart nicely. All of a sudden, the gang members came roaring through the door on their bikes with guns firing. The Recluse slammed on his brakes, and with machine gun in hand, he began mowing down bikers, one after another as they tried blasting their way past him. Some of their bullets hit but were quickly deflected by his suit. He dodged some with his lightning speed and instincts. If one of the gang members got by his machine gun, his trusty shotgun blew them away. Two shots fired, and the gun was reloaded in the blink of a tiger's eye.

The ground was full of downed gang members and motorcycles. One Saint ran toward him to attempt to physically take the Recluse on. Big mistake! The B.R. leapt off his bike and met him in midair. The biker swung a tremendous fist towards B.R., only to have his arm ripped completely off, and with one mighty blow from B.R.'s fist, he was knocked, dead, up against the side of the log barn.

As all of this was going down, Big Bubba and two others came flying out of the blasted door, and swiftly tore down the road. B.R. was on them like stink on a dead African hyena that has been baking in the sun for a week. He guessed that they were the only two remaining Satan's Saints, and that they were trying to protect the one in the middle, probably their leader. Reaching speeds over one hundred mph, they knew they were fleeing for their lives. Two out of the three dropped back and one turned a Thompson Machine Gun back toward B.R. and started firing. This was a stupid move. All he accomplished was putting bullet holes in the buildings, parked cars, and everything else on the street — everything but his target. He was trying to keep his motorcycle on the road, and he couldn't hit the side of a battleship.

B.R. calmly said, "Okay." Then he pulled his pistol from his side and with one shot, he took out the guy's back tire. The bike and rider went careening into a brick building splintering his neck. He never knew what hit him.

Down to two, the bikers and B.R. hit the I-80 bypass that went around and through Chicago. All lanes were full, and B.R. knew this was going to be a fun ride. These guys were ruthless police killers, and he wasn't letting up for nothing until they faced the judge, jury, and executioner.

Satan's Saints would soon know all about Satan for sure, but he wasn't too sure about the Saints. Weaving around cars, big rigs, and everything in between, the two frantically tried to lose the Recluse. The odds of that were zero with a capital Z. They'd become so desperate and reckless that the other cars were slowing down to get out of their way, which caused miles of wrecks and fender benders. B.R. with his ghost lights on made for an incredible sight in a driver's rearview mirror. He made everyone pull over to get out of the way.

The other biker tried again with his pistol to hit or at least slow B.R. down. At just the right moment, B.R. fired a single back tire shot, and nothing was left of the biker but a greasy spot on the freeway.

"So, this last guy must be the famous Big Bubba biker," B.R. assumed.

He had been prepped by Jarvis on how big and vicious Bubba was. Since Bubba hadn't fired a shot, though, B.R. decided to capture him for judgement day.

As they dashed through traffic, B.R. pulled alongside him, and getting as close as he could, he stuck both shotgun barrels against Bubba's temple and shouted, "Do you know that gospel song, Can't Nobody Do Me Like Jesus? If you don't stop that Harley, you won't have the chance to find out if it's true."

As he pulled back on the hammers, the engine of Bubba's bike began winding down, and he pulled over to the side of the road. When he stopped his Harley, he turned toward B.R. and said, "Do you think I can get a movie star to have sex with me?"

B.R. looked at him and said, "How in the hell would I —" BLAM!

Before B.R. could finish the statement, Big Bubba sucker punched him, but B.R. was full of venom and this just surprised him more than anything. Turning around, B.R. spit a mouthful of blood in Bubba's right eye. This infuriated Big Bubba, and he wound up for another blood gushing right hook. Just before his fist connected, B.R. caught it. He snapped that balled up fist back so hard that he pulled it clean off at the wrist. There was no fight left in Big Bubba, as he was screaming in pain. Pain like he had never felt.

B.R. tried to make a call to Jarvis to come pick Bubba up, but when Jarvis answered, all they could hear was Big Bubba's screams.

B.R. turned and politely said, "Do you mind? I'm trying to make a call, if you haven't noticed."

The rest of the policemen that had been shot survived, but a couple were injured so badly, they would have bone and muscle problems for life. Bubba was charged with murder, bank robbery, running from the law, sale of illegal drugs, prostitution, conspiracy, and everything else in between. He was headed for a hanging.

Back home, L.J. asked B.R, "With that many bikers, why didn't you get help from Bob and the other agents?"

B.R. replied, "They did help — they found the gang. That was the hard part. Besides, didn't the good guys win? Like I keep telling you, Samson killed one thousand soldiers with the jawbone of an ass, and I only had a few bikers to deal with. I want to go pay tribute to the families and friends of our fallen law comrades. That's what is most important to me."

Although the Chief agreed, he just shook his head. He knew the world had never seen anyone quite like B.R.

HAWAII

B.R. was given time off for some rest and relaxation. He decided to vacation in Hawaii, so he had to come up with a disguise so that no one would recognize him. His buddy and comrade Bob Jarvis came up with this nerdy outfit.

"Digging the spider guy as this brainy tourist. All you need is the white nose!"

Bob was the only one that could rib B.R. and get away with it, even though he always said, "I'm gonna get you back one of these days, mouth of the south."

A hat, eyeglasses, and wig did the trick. With that part taken care of, B.R. went to L.J. and said, "Look, I want to have some fun in Hawaii, and since I don't know anyone there, not even the guys within the FBI department, what if I took that crazy Bob Jarvis along with me? We could be Cheech and Chong, and he wouldn't even need a disguise."

The chief couldn't say no to the "secret weapon" of the FBI so he said, "Okay, now get the hell out of here, and don't call me when you run out of money."

B.R. grinned when Jarvis said, "Adios amigo."

Off to the 50th state they went.

They settled in Honolulu at a nice hotel on the beach. Looking out the window, B.R. could see the beauties in bikinis strolling beside the ocean.

"Man, they have some big waves here," Bob said.

"Big waves and look at all those gorgeous women. They are all here vacationing and looking for a good time, I hope," quipped B.R. "Oh yea! Let's check out the beach and then go out tonight for some fun," Bob said.

"I want to rent a surfboard and hit those waves. Maybe I can catch the eye of one of those good-looking girls," stated B.R.

"You want to take me on, surf boy?" Jarvis asked.

The two found a rental shop and got everything they needed to ride those famous waves.
Bob laughed and said, "I want to see you keep that wig and sunglasses on when a big wave wipes you out."

B.R. snarled, "Ain't no wave gonna wipe The Black Recluse out. And speak English. I can't understand that Spanish mumbo jumbo," B.R. teased.

Sure enough, the two rode waves for a good three hours, and B.R. never missed a ride. Bob wasn't half bad either, but he had been surfing before. It was B.R.'s first time and yea, the girls did notice that hunk of muscle killing those big waves. He was becoming more agile and athletic day by day. He would have even taken on a great white shark if he had been provoked by one.

B.R. was on the shore and the ladies surrounded him. They wanted to know all about him.

He told them, "I'm just a mountain boy from the hills of Tennessee."

With his hillbilly accent, the girls just wanted to hear him talk.

One lady in particular caught his eye, so he asked her to have dinner with him at the hotel he and Bob were staying in. There was a big Luau with Hawaiian dancers and music planned in the hotel courtyard. Tiki lights and bars were set up everywhere. The lady, who was a local, came to the Luau wearing a sexy grass skirt and blouse. When the music started, she started dancing and could flat shake her hips, to B.R.'s delight. Everything was going great for both Bob and B.R. until the loudspeakers in the courtyard blared out the news that there had been a volcano eruption on the Big Island. The Kilauea Volcano was spouting fire and rock high into the air. The lava flow had surrounded a small village, and everyone had been rescued except an elderly man and his young granddaughter. Attempts had been made, but the only way to rescue them was by helicopter, and it was impossible now because of the fire and rock exploding upward.

MOUTH OF A VOLCANO

When B.R. heard the situation, he immediately went into Black Recluse mode. He told Bob to communicate with the chopper crew.

"Tell them to attach the longest rescue cable that could be attached to the crank, and I will meet the chopper at the local airport in twenty minutes."

Bob called the fire department, identified himself, and said to have three sets of turnout gear at the airport — two for adults and a small one to use on the child — ASAP. Everyone would rendezvous with B.R. at the airport. He also asked for a parachute.

B.R., who was known as J.R. here on the island, said, "Excuse me," to his date and, in a wink, ran to the parking lot where he had seen someone's motorcycle. He quickly hot-wired it and, like a speeding bullet, he and Bob were off to the airport.

As they wheeled into the airfield, the chopper and firetruck were waiting for them. All they knew was that these two were F.B.I. agents, and they were prepared to help. Not having time to go into details, everyone just said I hope you know what you're doing and good luck. They had no idea what J.R. and Bob could do, but they had a feeling these two agents might be the only hope.

Once the helicopter was airborne, B.R. explained his plan to Bob, who was to man the winch for him. As they got closer to the Big Island, they could see the glow of fire and burning rocks of lava exploding into the air. B.R. was briefed on the almost impossible task at hand. The chopper would have to stay high enough to withstand the heat and rocks, and that meant the cable was the longest ever used in a rescue. They told both Bob and B.R. that the old man and child were in a concrete block utility house and that the lava was headed right for them.

J.R. borrowed a helmet and put on his turnout gear with the parachute strapped to his back. As the aircraft maneuvered through the smoke and ash, J.R. stared down toward the little village and spotted the block building where the two people were trying to survive. His sharp eyesight was a blessing in this critical situation.

B.R. told the pilot exactly where to hover so that he could exit in a free fall. The pilot was fighting the hot updraft as well as anyone could hope for as Bob dropped the door and told B.R. to get ready.

"I'll be saying a prayer for you my comrade," Bob said softly.

With everything set on go, J.R. leapt out of the helicopter into the hot ash carrying the two other sets of gear, dropping at speeds of over 100 m.p.h. straight down into the mouth of an erupting volcano.

His eagle eyes helped him dodge rocks and molten lava as he plunged downward. Down, down, down he glided, zig zagging toward that little building where there were two souls fearing death, not knowing the mighty spirit of a special man was on its way.

B.R. was 100 feet from the ground when he pulled the ripcord, and just before he crashed into the ground, his parachute opened — he gently stepped down to the earth. It was perfect timing in that hellish landscape of the volcano. B.R. jerked the parachute off, then raced to the metal door on the little building. With one powerful blow of his closed hand, he threw the metal door off its hinges. Cowered in the dark, the two trapped Hawaiians were so surprised.

B.R. grabbed them and said, "I am B.R., and I am going to get you to safety." Then he put the gear on the two terrified people.

Picking the child up with one arm and placing the old man on his back with his other, he raced out to the long, dangling wire cable that was flopping around in the heat and smoke from the eruptions.

"Hang on to me with everything you've got," he yelled over the noise of rock hitting the earth.

Grabbing the line with his bare hand, he gave it a jerk to signal Bob to kick the hoist into full throttle. As they ascended,

B.R. whipped around to take the hits, protecting the two from the rocks and lava that were flying toward them. His sixth senses were working overtime.

It seemed like an eternity, but finally, they were pulled the long, long distance up to the helicopter. As they entered, everyone breathed a sigh of relief.

The old man said, "God bless you. Are you an angel?"

B.R. responded, "No, I'm a long way from that, but thanks anyway. This is just something I was put on this earth to do.

Bob told B.R. he needed to get checked out. After some unkind words, B.R. finally agreed to let Bob look him over.

"This kind of beating would have finished off any other person, you ole son of a gun. This rubbing alcohol is going to hurt me more than it hurts you," Bob laughs.

"One of these days," was all B.R. could get out.

"Well, there went a hell of a good time back at the Luau, but you know what, it feels a whole lot better to do what we did," Bob said while holding the little girl.

WHAT'S NEXT

Back in Nashville, L.J. told his agents that B.R. only took thirty minutes to bring down The Glove, which would have taken them days normally — if they got him at all.

"Do you realize what we have in our arsenal?" he exclaimed. Everyone agreed and expressed gratitude to work with the Black Recluse. L.J. called a meeting later that day to go over the next assignment with B.R.

That night, everyone was on hand. Thinking about what they might hear made goosebumps stand on their arms in anticipation. Before the chief laid out the next job, he made a little toast to their "super-agent." B.R. appreciated it, but it made him feel a little embarrassed.

L.J. pulled out a bottle that was familiar to everyone.

"Since most of us are from Tennessee, it's only fitting to toast with something Tennessee made — Jack Daniels," Chief laughed.

"It's been a while since I've drank anything, but I think I can handle that," B.R. said.

L.J. replied, "I'm only agreeing to one drink. That's all I need — a room full of drunk law enforcement officers."

They all shouted in unison, "Ahh, Chief!" Then someone followed, "You sure know how to start and stop a party."

"The first thing I want to say before we talk about what lies before us is it's imperative that we continue to spread the rumor that B.R. is a ghost. It has to spread like a tidal wave crossing the ocean. Some people want to believe it, but a lot will need convincing. Humans are inquisitive about the unknown, especially the spirit of someone who violently died. It gives us a big edge in our fight against crime," explained L.J.

"Everyone has heard of Jack the Ripper, and if they haven't, they must have brain damage," chuckled L.J. Then his demeanor changed to a sober whisper. "We have word out of England that someone is slicing up women, and his calling card is that of Jack the Ripper! Some psychopath is imitating the original butcher," L.J. carefully explained.

"Scotland Yard has every British agent in London trying to come up with answers. They reported that it could be more than one person, and the Yard suspects cannibalism," said the chief.

England was notorious for dense fog, and with that kind of cover, it is tough to capture anything. Once again, prostitutes had been targeted, and these random females had been slaughtered. Brains and the upper thighs have been more popular, but all other organs had been taken out with surgical precision, just like the original killer. This made Scotland Yard suspect a surgeon.

L.J. explained how this info came into his hands from Washington.

"B.R. has been on the director's desk for a while now, and he knows everything about him, ghost and all. J. Edgar Hoover has been asked for support from Scotland Yard in this investigation. He thinks the Black Recluse with his superior strength, instincts, and vision might be the answer to dealing with the fog. What do you guys think?" L.J. inquired.

"Cannibalism? That makes me want to puke. You got my vote. When do we leave?" B.R. asked.

"I've never been to England, and I'd like to see the Beatles," the agent Bob Jarvis said.

"Everyone has many questions about how the F.B.I. would fit into a Yard case, I'm sure," said L.J.

He explained to the lawmen that B.R. could sense someone moving around in the foggy darkness from afar.

"That is the main reason we have been approached, and there have been sixteen women mutilated with not a legitimate clue as to who or where this person is hiding? Scotland Yard is working overtime and would accept our help gratefully."

Once it had been agreed on, everyone jumped into the game plan. They moved into London, secretly, and set up camp.

L.J. met with the top brass and was briefed on all the slayings, including when and where they had occurred on a large map of London.

Everyone was anxious to see B.R. operate. The Brass suggested giving him the layout of the murders, hoping that he would somehow instinctively find a pattern. Sure enough, after studying the killings, he began to see into the Ripper look-a-like's brain.

B.R. had been injected with so much spider venom that his normal heart rate was one hundred and fifty beats a minute. All of his senses were sharp as a straight razor, and he was getting a super rush by just thinking about how he would stalk this menace.

His brain had become a calculator, just like a spider knowing exactly where its prey was.

London was a city of eight million people, taking up six hundred square miles. Prostitution was legal, and there were seventy thousand registered girls in brothels and massage parlors. This many women on the streets and throwing the fog into the mix made for the perfect setup for someone like Jack the Ripper II.

B.R. dove into the info he had been briefed on. The Yard theorized that more than one person was involved, and the attacks came from overhead on the roofs. Houses and buildings in London are built side by side, and you could actually go block to block on their topside.

"Rope ladders would have to be used," B.R. figured.

After studying where the murders occurred, B.R. stood back away from the map of London, and a pattern began to emerge. Patterns were something he had long been a master of finding. Scotland Yard, and anyone else, hadn't been able to determine a pattern because it had appeared to be just random locations.

B.R. described his theory to L.J.

"Just picture how you tighten lug nuts on a car wheel. You start with one lug then go all the way across to tighten the second. The third nut is halfway between the first two, then go across to tighten the fourth lug nut. That leaves number five and six," explained B.R.

"Okay, what does that mean?" L.J. asked.

"To throw everyone off this simple pattern, the killers make it complicated by changing it up, making it look random. You start with lug one, then you go to the location of lug five to kill, but move the body to location number four. Next you go to location two, then to six, and move the body to location three. From this point, the kill is at location five, then at six," B.R. said.

"How do you know something that complicated is right?" L.J. asked.

"That's for me to know and for you to find out," laughed B.R.

"Seriously, Chief, the same pattern was used in the section of London where killings seven through twelve were discovered. Again, this pattern showed up in the third section of town where four women were dead and cut up, and I think we might have a shot at location five or hopefully six," B.R. theorized.

"Recluse, I have no clue how you came up with this pattern of killings, but I hope and pray you're right," L.J. cautiously said.

"These things just come to me," B.R. tried to explain.

"Alright, we need to zero in on the section of London you have determined will be next, and take this devil spawn out," L.J. angrily commanded.

Brothels were scattered throughout London, so it was literally searching for a needle in a haystack. A female "Bobbie" working for Scotland Yard volunteered to patrol the night streets as a hooker. Victoria was a black belt in karate and carried a pistol and sheathed knife under her skimpy outfit. She was a good-looking woman that had a fighting spirit of a pit bull.

She was equipped with a police radio to stay in constant contact with headquarters, and she would not be far away from Yard agents. They would act as ordinary Bobbies walking the beat.

Victoria had gotten to know and mingled with the prostitutes in the designated area that B.R. had determined. She soon fit right in, and no lady of the night had any idea she was a cop. Her assignment was to walk the streets and look for one or more persons that fit the M.O. of a killer. When she did get a proposal her excuse was, "You don't have enough money for my services, sweetheart. Find a girl that's more in your finances."

The rooftops were to be observed constantly, but that wasn't an easy thing to do in the fog.

B.R. would be close, sitting on his steel horse with all the lights off. He could navigate using his radar-like vision, even in the fog.

All of the details had been worked out and the plan was in motion, even though it was a long shot. Everyone was set to go, especially the Black Recluse!

Weather reports were saying heavy fog was moving in for the next few days. The order was given to roll on plan "widow maker." The night took on a creepy feeling as everyone took their positions in this unusual quest to catch a cannibalistic surgeon. B.R.'s heart was pounding in his brain. He was literally floating through the dark like a real ghost.

Part of the designated section had cobblestone roads with commercial buildings, pubs, market stores, and English style houses side by side. They utilized every square inch of real estate in that area.

Tori (Victoria) was street walking. She chatted now and then with the real walkers and the propositions she encountered. Everything was moving as planned, and nothing unusual gave any clues that this was going to be the night.

When the sun began its roll across the heavens, the Yard called everybody home. "We'll try again tomorrow night," was the consensual agreement, although B.R. was extremely disappointed. After all, it was his theory, and he didn't like to be wrong. He lived by that old saying, "I might not always be right, but you can take it to the bank — I ain't never wrong."

L.J. calmed him down as he explained, "It's only the first night. What do you want, to be a genius on the first go around?"

Tori realized after that night what a dangerous assignment she had agreed to do, but figured, "I'm more prepared than those other girls will ever be!"

The second night came and went, then the third and fourth nights passed without a sign of anything unusual. Just the regular interactions of English lifestyle. Scotland Yard began to question B.R.'s judgement, but L.J. and the boys held true to the theory. Bob Jarvis, one of the most rambunctious of the agents whom B.R. had taken a liking to, confronted the Yard by saying, "I'd bet my F.B.I. badge that my good friend is right."

One thing was for sure — the fog was rolling in as forecasted even during daylight hours. After twelve nights on the streets, B.R. told everyone he had a strong feeling that, "Time is getting real close because tomorrow night will be a full moon and my senses are in overdrive."

Everyone made sure that they were well rested and ready for twilight. As the sun sunk below the horizon, the moon climbed into the Eastern sky. Fog had a mysterious effect on most people, but with the moonlight thrown in, it was like being on some strange, far away planet.

Once again, everyone was in place, cautiously anticipating a "strike." B.R. was slowly motoring through the glowing fog. Tori, working the streets from pub to brothel said, "Nothing yet."

As she walked toward a narrow back alley, something or someone caused the fog to slightly swirl and her "claws" automatically sprang into action.

As she said, "Maybe," on the radio, the night exploded. Instantly, she was surrounded by three men, all wearing black trench coats with hats pulled low over their foreheads.

"Are you boys looking for a good time?" Tori asked with a sexy tone.

"We've been waiting for you, and you only," one dude said with an unfamiliar accent.

He was a giant of a man and had no idea she was law enforcement. As he and his cohorts put their hands on her, they were surprised. After grabbing her arms, the big dude felt a sharp pain in his gonads. Tori had unleashed a lightning quick knee-kick square between his legs. With him bending over in severe pain, Tori did a spinning back-kick to the second guys face, breaking his nose. BAM, BAM — and two of them were disabled that quick.

Hearing the situation coming from her radio, B.R. went into attack mode along with the Yard agents, but things turned ugly — fast.

Even though B.R. was almost there, the third person pulled out an old-fashioned blow stick that shot a dartlike arrow. He blew into it and hit Tori in the neck. It was poison-tipped and deadly. She dropped instantly, something Scotland Yard didn't see coming.

The hollow blow stick was used because it was silent unlike a gunshot. That was how they had been so successful with hiding their killings.

Tori was dead in less than a minute. The other two got their bearings, picked Tori up, and headed to a rope ladder that was hanging from a rooftop.
Abruptly, the apparent leader of the three said, "Leave her — she's a spy. It was a setup."

In their rush, they left Victoria with the dart still in her neck. The autopsies hadn't been able to determine the cause of the other deaths. The cause, as Scotland Yard would now find out, was poison from a bird found only in New Guinea called a Pitohui. Its feathers secreted the most deadly poison on earth known as a Batrachotoxin. These birds created it from eating poison frogs. New Guinea was also a place where cannibalism was still practiced.

Things were beginning to fall into place.

As the three men climbed the ladder, B.R. arrived on the scene. He saw the killers on top of the roof. He quickly checked Tori and realized she had paid the ultimate price for doing her job. Anger pushed the venom filled blood through his shaking body, and fire flashed from his eyes. Her death left him feeling guilty. That brought him to the point of going absolutely crazy.

"Those sons of bitches are going to have hell to pay! I'm gonna rip their hearts out with my bare hands!" B.R. screamed.

Jumping on his motorcycle, like a cowboy jumping on a horse, he was in hot pursuit with his eagle eyesight following the black clothed figures running on the roof tops. They went from building to building then disappeared down the backside of an old warehouse.

B.R. circled the building in time to see a black Rolls Royce streaking away down a cobblestone road. He turned on the ghost lights and gave chase. Left, then right, the car turned onto adjoining streets trying to lose the eerie aberration glued to their rear end.

Machine guns began firing from the back windows. His bulletproof windshield was deflecting them. He flipped a switch that activated his machine gun and began ripping the back of the Rolls to shreds.

Suddenly, the car shot into a garage door that had been electronically opened by the killers. The door closed as fast as it opened. Again, B.R. flipped a switch. This one activated his rocket launchers. He fired two missiles and blew the door, and part of the building, to smithereens. He did this without slowing down and continued to jet into the smoking cavern. As B.R. roared through the smoke, he locked his brakes down and screeched to a sideways halt. Bright spotlights shone down on him and it took a moment for him to focus his vision.

Three figures walked out of the backroom and one said, "Whom do I have the pleasure of meeting?"

B.R. instantly recognized the British accent. He also realized that these butchers were equipped for this kind of encounter and loaded with weaponry.

He played the game and said, "They call me the Black Recluse, and I'm a ghost spirit from the other side. Let me guess — you are Jack the Ripper, and these two punks are your assistants?"

"You know my name, but I don't believe in ghosts," said Jack.

Then he told his cronies to see if he truly was spirit or human. Like a true gunfighter, B.R. drew his pistol, shot out the spotlights, and flipped off his suit's ghost lights quick as a heartbeat. The big man stepped toward the spot B.R. was standing and fired his automatic gun through the dark. At that moment, he felt a tap on his shoulder and instinctively turned in the dark. An elbow from B.R. landed on his mouth, knocking him backward.

"Get him!" shouted Jack, and the other thug whacked B.R. in the head with his gun barrel.

With his helmet taking the blow, this only infuriated the Black Recluse more. He made the old Turkey Doll screech and straight kicked him in the knee, breaking his leg. Down he went.

The Ripper started firing his weapon toward the sound, but B.R. wasn't there. He could see them, but they couldn't see him. Big boy, back on his feet and firing his gun wildly, brought a shout from Jack, "Don't kill me, you idiot.!"

B.R. reached and grabbed the gun barrel, and with one karate chop to the windpipe, shattered his throat. Big man's heart was pumping erratically, but no oxygen could reach his brain. He flopped over, his heart beating no more.

Ole broke leg fired frantically in the direction of the noise.

"Ah hell," B.R. said impatiently. He pulled his double barrel shotgun out and put this serial killer out of his misery.

"Well, well. Looks like bad ass Jack the Ripper has lost two assistants, and now it's just you and me," B.R. bragged with that haunting laugh. His ghost lights made the large room glow like an Egyptian tomb. He saw Jack trying to hide behind his Rolls Royce.

"Tell you what, I'm going to spare your life. Just tell me why you are doing the things you do." B.R. said.

"I guess you are a ghost or something like one, but it's still hard for me to accept. I haven't figured it out yet, but if you will let me go, I'll explain my enterprises. Do we have a deal? I will leave England and disappear," Jack nervously pleaded.

"Maybe so, but you better hurry. Scotland Yard will be crawling all over this place very soon," B.R. answered.

He wasn't sure Jack believed him, but the Ripper didn't have much of a choice. Little did he know Jack only agreed because he had an ace up his sleeve.

Again, Jack asked him, "Why would you do this for me?"

B.R. assured him saying, "For some weird reason, I want to see what goes on in a sick brain like yours."

"Follow me and I'm going to show you something only three people have seen, and two are dead," Jack confessed.

At the back of the room, Jack touched a secret switch and two doors in the floor slid open. A long passageway disappeared into the dark hole.

"Very clever," said B.R. Jack flipped on a light switch, and B.R. was shocked at what he saw.

"I've just entered the laboratory of an alien spacecraft," he theorized.

"Welcome to my world, Black Recluse. I can understand why you are intrigued by me. I know an inquisitive mind when I see one, and you have one," Jack explained. He took off his coat and hat and slipped into a doctor's lab suit.

"He looks like an alien with that bald head and facial features. Man, what an ugly son of a bitch, but why is he being so agreeable?" B.R. asked himself.

"Let me tell you my story. I've been longing to share this with someone from outside of my world, and it has to be, well, a ghost," The Ripper explained.

"Let's check out my house," Jack laughed.

B.R. looked at all the scientific glass containers and machines that were attached to one another, and he was grossed out by all the human organs inside of them.

"Yes, there are lungs, livers, kidneys, and brains all at my disposal. I'm a fabulous surgeon that is involved with black market human organs. I make a hundred times more money doing this than doing surgery," stated Jack.

"So, you call yourself Jack the Ripper to throw the law dogs off, right?" B.R. asked.

"Of course, my observant spider," teased Jack.

"What is this rumor of cannibalism?" B.R. asked, disgusted.

"Ah yes, would you care to taste some human brains? I have the best recipe. It was taught to me by the Korowai Tribe in New Guinea. I went there as a British missionary, but I came back with a craving to dine on human brains. It is delicious and, oh yes, human thighs are just out of this world," The Ripper evilly spewed.

"You sick asshole, you're going to see the first ghost to ever puke. Well, I wanted to know what makes a person do such unthinkable inhumanities, and now I know. You have got to be the rottenest snake I've ever encountered," snarled B.R.

"Life is all about how you perceive it. Everybody lives their lives differently. I'm also an atheist that believes in reincarnation," Jack explained.

"Now I know your brains are scrambled, but to each his own," B.R. replied.

Suddenly, the spider senses told him this guy's demeanor was about to reveal something different. He could tell things were about to change.

"What in tarnation is your real name? Might as well tell me since you've told me your life story," said B.R.

"My name is Attila the Hun," laughed Jack.

"Of all the comedians in the world, you've got to be the worst," B.R. angrily smarted off, starting to lose his patience.

"Let me ask you a question, I think I already know the answer though. I'm betting you have sex with dead girls, too," B.R. said.

"Oh man, sex with a corpse is the ultimate mental ecstasy in the world. It's pure euphoria," Jack relished.

"When you do get caught, the judge is going to sentence you to thirty days in the British electric chair, and there won't be anything left of you but a figment of everyone's imagination," B.R. quipped.

"You think so, huh? Let me show you one of my prized possessions that I picked up in the Amazon Jungle," Jack calmly said.

He opened a drawer and gingerly unwrapped a human head. Amazingly, it was shrunk down to just a fraction of a normal one.

Before Jack had gotten the shrunken head out of the drawer, he had slipped a dagger into one sleeve of his lab coat and a Derringer pistol in the other. B.R.'s sixth sense had already sounded the alarm, and he had been following every move Jack made.

"Isn't this the damnedest thing," said Jack. He handed the head to B.R. making sure he took it with his right hand. At the exact same moment B.R. took that hideous thing, the Ripper triggered a spring that shot the dagger out to his right hand. He lunged at the Black Recluse to plunge it deep in his gut, but

B.R. was way too clever for such a silly move by Jack.

B.R. smacked Jack's arm with such force that it cracked the bones, and Jack howled with pain. Then B.R. smashed that shrunken head on Jack's face, knocking him backward.

The next mistake ole Ripper made was springing the pistol out and shooting B.R. square at his heart. The bulletproof suit just repelled the shot. As far as Jack knew, it had just passed through B.R.'s body.

"I can't believe it. If you really are a spirit, just what kind of a ghost are you?" Jack asked pathetically.

B.R. slowly pulled his shotgun out and said, "This is for Victoria, that woman you left lying in the street!"

He cocked both barrels and pointed the gun at Jack's face.

"Wait a minute, you made a vow to let me leave England if I told you everything!" cried Jack.

With that classic grin, the Black Recluse yelled, "I LIED!"

The last words Jack the Ripper II ever heard was the Black Recluse saying, "Arrivederci, you scum sucking slug!"

Then both barrels separated his head from his body.

REFLECTING

Midnight, with a full moon found B.R. on top of a mountain close to Kantrell Crossing. Yes, J.R. had gone back home, but he was alone. He wasn't allowed to be seen by anyone except his mother and father. His soul purpose of coming back was to have a quiet place and some time to contemplate what the hell his life had become.

B.R. missed his old friends and the other members of his family.

"Did I make the right decisions?" he pondered.

Across the moon, he saw bats flying around, catching insects, and even an owl darting here and there, catching its prey. He rationalized that this is what his existence had become. On the other hand, if these opportunities hadn't come his way then he would have been on the other side of the law, maybe even in jail. Deep in his heart, he knew he did make the right decision, even though it did get lonely sometimes.

The F.B.I. Agency considered him to be their top agent or you could say, "incredible weapon."

He had continued to get stronger, faster, and more cunning.

B.R. was literally becoming a Super Cop, and that was not a comic book acknowledgment! The spider venom had definitely created a new J.R. Dawkins, and whether he liked it or not, it is who he had become.

The main reason the Black Recluse was sitting on a dirt bike high on a Tennessee hill is that he had noticed something that had him extremely confused about his future. Something that had hit him like a freight train.

He wasn't aging like a normal man.

B.R. had started to notice that his coworkers and parents were growing older, but he wasn't. All he had to do was look in the mirror. If his observation was correct, how long did that mean his life was going to be? One hundred, two hundred? He had no clue how long he would live, and this kicked his imagination into overdrive.

"Am I going to turn into an actual spider?" he laughed.

Getting serious with himself, he began wondering what laid ahead in his future.

"What will it be like in 1988 and on into 1998? What will the lifestyles be like in that next century?"

B.R. let his mind visualize ahead to 2018 and beyond.

"What will trains, planes, cars, and especially motorcycles be like?"

He got a rush thinking about it.

"If I am correct and I do not age normally, I guess I'd better start preparing for my future assignments."

Move over James Bond!

The Black Recluse is
here to stay!

J. EDGAR HOOVER

Monday morning finds The Black Recluse sleeping late, but then he prepares his itinerary for a meeting with the F.B.I. chief at 3:00 p.m. in Nashville, Tennessee. He has been told by his superior that important information has been sent from the big boss man Herbert Hoover in Washington. B.R. was thinking, "I wonder what he wants to talk to me about? Oh well, I've always wanted to meet the man."

B.R. arrives around 2:45 at the state headquarters and is met by L.J. and a couple of ranking F.B.I. officials. Quickly getting down to business, the Chief explains to the small group that Mr. Hoover wants B.R. in D.C. by tomorrow for a top-secret meeting, and that was the extent of the conversation. L.J. told B.R. that was about all he could say at this time.

The plane sits down around 10 o'clock in Washington, and

B.R. is escorted to a limo waiting at the airport. After a thirty- minute ride, he arrives at F.B.I. International Headquarters and is hurriedly rushed to the office of J. Edgar Hoover. B.R. is disguised as usual, so no one knows this person that is entering the building.

Reaching the office of the director, B.R. smells the scent of pipe tobacco. As he enters, J. Edgar stands up with pipe in mouth and extends his hand to the Black Recluse.

"So, I finally get to meet this mysterious creation of a powerful man that I have been hearing so much about, " Mr. Hoover booms vocally.

B.R. realizes who the "boss" is.

"Nice to me you sir," B.R. replies.

"Let's get down to brass tacks. Word has got to me that we have a situation bordering on the supernatural, if you can believe such a thing, and I'm not sure I can believe such stuff," the director confesses.

"What do you mean, supernatural?" B.R. asked.

"Somewhere in California there are whispers getting to me of a preposterous story about a wolfman creature terrorizing a mountainous area. We can't let this get out because it would create havoc in the media and fear in the locals. That's why I summoned you to D.C. and formed a plan with you in charge since you seem to be about as crazy as a wolfman. Whose idea was it to call you a black recluse, let alone a ghost?" J. Edgar laughs.

"Piece of cake," B.R. grins.

"Well, I'm glad you're so confident, even though your record has been something out of the twilight zone," J. Edgar admits.

After talking about some other "problems" the F.B.I. had for B.R., the director told him to get back with him on the California situation when he studied it and had a plan. With that, B.R. was off to Nashville to see what was in store for his upcoming mission.

PRISON BREAK

J.R. Dawkins was pumping iron and shooting up spider venom at an unbelievable amount. He was developing into a "monster" of a man. Strength and agility were exploding, and there wasn't a single fat cell in his chromosomes, just raw muscle with that uncanny sixth sense. The F.B.I. knew they had an incredible fighting machine at their disposal. With all the comic book superheroes that people of all ages loved to read about, no one had ever dreamed someone human could be compared to them in their made-up crime fighting world of fantasy.

Working at the Nashville Headquarters late one night, a call came into the office and an agent screamed, "Where is the Chief?"

Holding the phone, he tells everyone in hearing distance that there has been a prison break at the Federal Penitentiary in the town of Petros, Tennessee. This is where the Brushy Mountain State Penitentiary Correction Complex is located. It is a large maximum-security prison operated by the Tennessee Department of Corrections.

"The Chief is taking in a hockey game," someone yelled.

"Well, go get him," said the agent with the phone. Then he tells everyone in the office that an accomplice of James Earl Ray, convicted killer of Dr. Martin Luther King, and five more convicts have escaped. The alarm hits the air waves, and L.J. is informed. He calls a meeting at the headquarters and contacts B.R. to rush his butt to the meeting ASAP.

The Black Recluse had already heard the news on his police scanner and knew what was going down. He gathers his outfit, clothes, and everything he would need to hit the Cumberland Mountains in Petros.

As the F.B.I. agents gather at headquarters, plans were quickly put in place. The Chief tells B.R. and one other agent to take the assignment. B.R. called for a helicopter to take his gear and specially built dirt bike to the landing platform where they would board. The trip was 150 miles away and only took less than an hour to the prison. They were up and away 30 minutes after the meeting.

The accomplice, nicknamed Flyboy, and the five prisoners had hacksawed their way out into the courtyard where they hid a homemade ladder made from lightning wire conduit to scale over the wall. Once they hit the woods, all six scattered up the surrounding mountains. When the prison guards realized they had escaped, the chase was on. Policemen, prison guards, and F.B.I. were all involved in the manhunt. By the time everyone was ready to go, The Black Recluse pulls up on his bike looking like the ghost he purposely was portraying. Everyone there had heard of the Recluse, but seeing him in person was an awesome image burned into their brains. Within a moment, the ghost was gone headed for the mountains. With his super senses, he could tell where the escapees had started their mad scramble to flee through briars and brambles up the mountain side. He could see the trails through the bushes and trees like no other human would be able to see.

Picking a trail at random, B.R. throttles his machine through and around the rugged mountain terrain in hot pursuit of a "runner." With that "silent" muffler on his cycle, you couldn't hear him climbing the rugged mountain.

The Cumberland Plateau is a chain of mountains north of the great Smokies, and the area between the two is called the Tennessee Valley. There are places in the Cumberland range called The Little Grand Canyon. Big South Fork National Park is second to the Smokies in size.

As B.R. weaves his way up the mountain, he encounters all forms of rock and crevice formations. When he comes to one of the large crevices, he guns his engine — only someone with his skills as a bike rider would even consider the jump. In the dark he goes airborne, dodging trees as he flies by, but safely comes down on the other side. That crevice had to be one hundred feet deep.

SANDY AND LITTLE RED

Picking up the trail again, he can tell by the brush the prisoner is near. Slowing and picking his way, B.R. motors around the guy and stops. Soon, he hears the heavy breathing of a man headed toward him. Illuminating in the dark like the ghost he portrays, the prisoner's eyes focus on the scary aberration of a creature on the mountain. The Black Recluse introduces himself, then whacks him across the face with that sawed-off shotgun. Gave him a sleeping pill, you might say! After stringing him up in a rope spider web, B.R. is off to the next "prey." As he cuts across the side of the mountain, he can hear the blood hounds on a chase after another runner, so he calculates where a third person is fleeing. With his senses sharp as a wizard, he soon picks up another trail.

He climbs up to a thicket so dense he knows the only way through would be over the top. Eyeing the situation, he sees a rise and a huge rock formation close to the cluster of thorns. Throttle twisted wide open, he hits the rise and goes airborne again and lands on the boulder, where he takes to the air once more over the impregnable mass of flesh-ripping vegetation. With that done, one more time he is on the next hunt for a prisoner.

"This guy must be a 'running fool' because this trail leads higher and higher up this steep mountain. A whole lot further than the first man got," B.R. says to himself.

Trees and brush get even thicker, if you can believe such a thing, so B.R. slows a little to penetrate these woods. Big fir trees with limbs all the way to the ground are one reason he changes his speed.

Eventually, he realizes the runner is not far away.

Just like the first prisoner, B.R. does his thing. Walking down in front of the guy with his outfit all lit up, he gives the prisoner a big grin and says, "I bet you could win a marathon with your kind of running speed. I know you could use a long, cold drink of water from one of these mountain streams. Yum, yum!"

Suddenly, the muscular prisoner swings a huge piece of limb at The Recluse's head, only to find it lands in the Spider's hand.

"Bad decision," B.R. states, and with that, he rips the limb out of his hands and punches him in the gonads with it. The prisoner could hardly breath from the sharp pain between his legs. Up he goes in The Black Recluse's rope web. Number two was like a fly in a hanging position.

B.R. radios the other cops to see if their prognosis was successful.

"We have tracked down two escapees with two to go, and Flyboy is one of them," they said.

"Sounds like the spot on blood hounds Sandy and Little Red are earning their dog chow tonight, " B.R. laughs.

"Yea, but if we don't get Flyboy, there could be a nationwide revolt, " says the other F.B.I. agent.

"No worries, I didn't come here to just go mountain climbing," quips B.R.

With only two left to capture, B.R. cuts across the mountain side and in the distance, he hears the blood hounds picking up another scent, so he angles in a direction that determines where the last person must be located. Sure enough, his calculations are right. Criss-crossing for a while, he sees a trail left by a human. The problem is that it's getting daylight, and the dogs have stopped barking. Once again, he calls the other agent and discusses the changing situation. For some reason the trails have turned cold, so they decide to sit tight and reevaluate this problem. After giving it a long thought, they figure somehow the two remaining prisoners have hid out and, by not moving, have lessened the tracking.

"Let's wait till dark and see if they go on the move," the agent considers.

"May not be a bad idea," B.R. says and tells him to stay in touch.

The Recluse goes into survival mode and spots two squirrels in a large acorn tree. He quickly scales it and swings around the limbs to catch both. Ripping fur off and gutting the rodents, he washes them in a small creek flowing down the mountain. Eating the squirrels raw, he thinks to himself, "Not bad. It ain't pheasant, but will do," he determines. After finding a pile of leaves, he lays horizontal for some shut eye.

While sleeping, a big black bear comes up to the Recluse but snorts and hurries away. It can sense that he is something not to mess with. Animals are very intelligent in a lot of natural ways. A copperhead snake does the very same thing and slithers away.

As twilight time approaches and the halfmoon

appears over the horizon, he hears his radio squawk.

"The hounds are becoming excited. I think the prisoners are on the move," says the agent.

"I'm off to capture," he states, and with that off into the darkness speeds The Black Recluse.

Zig-zagging again for the last time, he tackles the rugged terrain looking for a clue to the whereabouts of the last two prisoners. After almost an hour, he comes to a spot where a dead skunk had been killed recently.

"A-Ha, so that's how the convict got some rest without dogs on his tail. No one or no 'thing' wants to get within a mile of that skunk smell, even me," he laughs, knowing it's going to be hard to even get near that God-forsaken man, but life is not promised to smell like roses!

He can see where the "big smell" has run off up the mountain, and he has been running in a creek that comes down the mountain side.

"Smart, and hard to follow, but I can trail that skunk smell," he chuckles.

Up the creek, the Recluse rides as the smell continues to get closer. He wraps part of his red scarf around his face to cut down that smell.

Stopping his bike, he breaks a long piece of a sapling tree to use as a weapon. Sure enough, the man is standing knee deep in the creek with a huge boulder in his hand.

"I've heard stories about you, and I ain't afraid of

no ghost," the prisoner growls.

"Well guess what? I ain't afraid of no ghost either, cause I'm the baddest ghost around here," The Black Recluse says.

The convict heaves the heavy boulder at him like it weighed nothing. He blocks the rock with the end of the pole, and fast as a mad hornet, he smashes the guy right between the eyes with the same pole end, nearly poking out his brains. Down he goes and is left hanging between two trees.

"Talk about not touching someone with a ten-foot pole," he laughs.

Meanwhile, Sandy and Little Red had been on the scent of the last prisoner, which was Flyboy. The two blood hounds followed the scent up to the peak of the mountain where they started howling in a frenzy. About fifteen cops circled the area, which was covered with leaves. Using high powered flash-lights, they see a hand and a foot sticking out of the leaves, and one cop said, "Is that you Mr. Fly-Poop?"

Slowly, the leaves move and up stands the noto-rious killer. He was completely covered in mud, sweat, and leaves — almost unrecognizable. The great prison break was over.

Back in Nashville at headquarters, once again the chief had a little toast to B.R. and agent.

"Well done. You two and all those law enforcement officers held in check what could have turned into a very ugly situation in this United States of America.

Flyboy would have been a big problem!"

Everyone was told James Earl Ray acted alone, but the conspiracy had been covered up. Flyboy got his name flying cocaine out of Colombia.

COCAINE

Chief L.J. met with B.R. a couple of days after he returned to discuss what Director J. Edgar had said about the rumors and stories of a wolf creature in California.

"I'd love to go after a 'werewolf' if there really was such a thing," B.R. said.

"Well, I haven't heard nothing else about it, and if I do, you'll be the first to know," laughs the Chief.

While studying the layout of the Amazon jungle, B.R. ran across the subject of headhunters. This brought back memories of London, England and the Jack the Ripper copycat. His curiosity got the best of him, so he checked how and why natives kill and shrink people's heads.

Several tribes of the Jivaroan group — including the Shuar in eastern Ecuador and northern Peru along the rivers Chinchipe, Bobonaza, Morona, Upand, and Pastaza, main tributaries of the Amazon river — practiced headhunting for trophies. The heads were shrunk and were known locally as tzan-tzas. B.R. studied their methods of how to shrink a head.

First the skin and hair are separated from the skull to allow them to shrink at different rates. Then the eyelids are sewn shut and the mouth is stuck closed with a peg. For the actual shrinking, the head is placed in a big pot and boiled for a very specific amount of time.

Once removed from the pot, the head would be 1/3 its original size, and the skin dark and rubbery. The skin would then be turned inside out, and any leftover flesh scraped off with a knife. The scraped skin was then turned with the proper side out again, and the slit in the rear sewn together.

The head was shrunk even further by inserting hot stones and sand to make it connect from the inside. This also "tanned" the inside, like tanning an animal hide, in order to preserve it.

Once the head reached the desired size and is full of small stones and sand, more hot stones would be applied to the face to seal and shape the features. The skin was rubbed with charcoal ash to darken it and, as tribesmen believed, to keep the avenging soul from seeping out. The finished product was hung over a fire to harden and blacken, then the wooden pegs in the lips pulled out and replaced with string to lash them together.

"Well, that's how it's done by those creepy sons-a-bitches," B.R. said to himself. He almost lost his lunch eaten earlier.

BOREDOM TO ACTION

After a few weeks doing this type of analysis on crime activity, B.R. was getting restless. He was almost to the point of telling the chief to get him on an assignment before he goes nuts.

He had been staying in the gym quite a bit more than usual, and his muscles and strength were erupting. The recluse venom was being injected "overtime." This crazy combination of venom and human blood was still a mystery that no one had figured out at this time!

After a couple of days with his head inside a pile of books studying a crime, L.J. suddenly burst in and said, "I know you are dying to get on your steel horse so guess what, I've been in touch with Mr. Hoover about the spooky rumors of a wolf-type person or animal in California, but I've got something 'hot' I need you to jump on ASAP."

"Oh, thank the Lord! What you got cookin' boss?" says B.R.

"One of our Amazon native informants that was busted a year ago tells us how Sergio Slasher Mendez's gang is transporting pink cocaine out of Peru," L.J. explains.

B.R. follows up saying, "It must be good, 'cause I can see you're excited."

The chief and B.R. begin their assignment plans for this FBI drug war.

"Seems that some native down in Peru accidently discovered a cave in a ridiculously dense section of the jungle that nobody knew anything about. It led down underground to a huge river that ran beneath the Amazon River," L.J. explains.

Somehow the Slasher cartel was using crude two-man submarines to haul the pink coke to the Atlantic Ocean.

The chief told B.R., "I want you to study everything you can get your hands on about the Amazon River, Colombia, and Peru."

"You got it, Chief," B.R. promises.

With that said, B.R. dives into the Amazon project... and this is what he discovers.

PINK COCAINE

The Amazon River starts from the Montaro River, and it is 3,977 miles long. It's the largest river by discharge volume of fresh water in the world, and by some definitions it is the longest. It discharges 7,831,000 cubic feet into the Atlantic Ocean every second. It runs through Brazil, Colombia, and Peru. Its basin is home to the Amazon rain forest, the world's richest and most varied biological reservoir. There are no bridges across the river. The only way to cross is by boat.

The river is home to a dolphin that blushes itself pink. It's called the Boto, the largest dolphin in the world.

This river supplies the earth with 20% of its freshwater supply. As it pours into the Atlantic Ocean, the freshwater persists over an area of 2.5 million square kilometers.

The rain forest is home to more than 40,000 species of flora, 2,000 species of fish, over 400 species of both mammals and amphibians, and 2.5 million insects.

The largest and most feared predator is the black caiman. You would think it would be piranha or the anaconda. Resembling an alligator (only far bigger and scarier) the black caiman is the largest predator living in the river. It eats anything — including humans.

The bull shark, known in the saltwater oceans, also lives in the Amazon River. It has adapted to the freshwater somehow.

The most unusual thing B.R. discovers is that there is a river which flows beneath the Amazon River, and it has been unknown except for a few jungle natives that happened to find it going exploring down in a cave. It is in a part of the jungle that is so dense no one could get through — except one determined native! They kept it a secret.

This underground river follows the path of the Amazon River for its entire length, approximately 6,000 kms. They named it Rio Hamza and it is "hundreds" of times wider than the Amazon.

Somehow, word from the natives that discovered this underground river got to the pink cocaine cartel so B.R. starts putting two and two together.

"That's how they move the pink stuff in those two-man submarines. It's completely oblivious to the world moving it underground," he states.
The thought of this wild setup in the Amazon Jungle has got the Recluse extremely excited.

"This is going to be one freaky, adventurous drug bust," B.R. tells his close friend, agent Bob Jarvis.

RIDING THE AMAZON

Two weeks later, B.R., Bob Jarvis, and the FBI native informant (who works for them now) are preparing to navigate down the Amazon River. A steam-powered 25 foot flat-bottom boat has been secretly shipped to Lima, Peru, which is the capital city of over eight million people. It lies on the country's arid Pacific coast.

The boat was trucked to headwaters of the Amazon River where B.R. had calculated the vicinity of the secret cave that leads to the underground river.

"The operators of the small subs have to surface periodically to resupply air," B.R. tells Bob.

What they didn't know was how many natives lost their lives exploring this incredible underground "wonder." Dozens of locals faced the challenge and wound up drowning. Finally, they did discover air-filled caves down the river all the way to the Atlantic Ocean. The drug runners now had a preposterous means of moving this pink cocaine, and the Slasher cartel was in total control.

The studies indicated that Sergio (Slasher) Mendez was the main cartel boss of this coke. He got his nickname Slasher when he caught someone snitching or stealing from his cocaine empire. He would tie their hands and take them to the middle of the Amazon River. Once there, he had a razor-sharp long knife that he used to slash wounds all over their naked body, women or men. As the blood poured, Sergio would say, "Swim as fast as you can to the closest bank, and you might survive."

He knew that couldn't be done because the piranha, smelling the captive's blood, would be there in a heartbeat. With an evil laugh, Sergio would push them out of the boat and into the piranha infested waters where they would be begging and screaming for their lives trying to swim with hands tied.

Out of nowhere the piranha would swarm a bloody body, snapping and ripping every ounce of flesh, eyeballs, and brains from the skeleton. Within two minutes, nothing but bones and hair were all that was left of a human body. Sometimes a black caiman alligator would snatch the victim from the piranha and eat it — bone and all. Mercy, what a gruesome way to die!

SEARCHING FOR CAVES

B.R. and Bob had everything packed on the boat, which had a small cabin on board where they carried supplies and hammocks to sleep on. B.R. had his mountain bike and Recluse outfit to use when needed. He calculated sooner or later he would find the smuggler's route.

"Let's eradicate some pink stuff," Bob chuckled, and off they motored with steam puffing from the engine stack. The steam engine could run by burning logs and sticks gathered from the forest.

B.R. was hoping to find the main cave entrance, but being 4,000 miles long, this would be a difficult achievement.

The first two days were uneventful — not a soul was seen on the river or riverbanks.

"The entrance to a cave has got to be close on these banks, but man this jungle is dense," Bob exclaimed.

About every half mile, B.R., Bob, and the informant guide would dock and search the area for any sign of a cave opening. The mosquitoes and bugs were ridiculous, although they had repellent. The guide knew which jungle plant could be used to repel the blood suckers, and that was good to know if needed. Being born and raised in the rain forest, the guide knew a bunch about survival.

On the third day as they were passing under a grove of rubber trees, something set B.R.'s sixth sense in panic mode. Suddenly, a huge anaconda big enough to swallow a man dropped down from a tree and landed on Bob, unexpectedly. Quick as a wink, the snake curled around him and was aiming the mouth toward Bob's head. To the anaconda's surprise, his mouth landed on a hand that is mightier than a bear trap. B.R. rammed his left fist down the snake's throat, and with his right hand grasp the huge varmint near its eyes. With a mighty squeeze, B.R. popped that snake's eyeballs completely out, then he took both hands and stretched its neck and head totally away from its body.

Bob yelled, "Get this bastard off me, please!"

B.R. told the guide to uncurl the snake from around Bob's body, giving out a little chuckle.

"Better watch out for hob goblins," B.R. laughed.

"Thanks, but that ain't funny," Bob replied. "Lord help me if B.R. wasn't here," he thought to himself.

Searching for the entrance cave to the underground river was like a needle in a haystack. A map was drawn at each mile of the Amazon River so they wouldn't double track themselves. A slow and uncertain job, but B.R. never wavered on his instincts.

"It's here within a few miles," he said.

Sergio Mendez and his gang continuously stay on the move through the jungle making it almost impossible to pin him down.

Finally, the day came when B.R.'s deductions paid off. Hacking their way through dense underbrush to an opening in this jungle flora, B.R. could sense a path faintly visible to him. Following it for a short distance, he could tell by tree branches and leaves something was purposely covered up. They had found the entrance cave, and it was like a gold strike!

The mouth of the cave had been dug out to move equipment and cocaine down to the underground river. B.R. could tell it had been used a day or two earlier and knew a load of coke was being submarined downstream.

Their presence at the cave was not a complete secret. Word travels in the jungle in many mysterious ways, and B.R. knew this. Dropping down inside the cave with a long rope, B.R. explores the way down to the water. He takes in this magnificent sight of the underground river, something not many eyes have ever seen.

"Unbelievable," he says to himself.

The cave walls had crevices with long crystal stalagmites and stalactites that reflected in the beautiful blue water. A color that isn't present on the earth's surface.

With only his waterproof flashlight and the vision of an eagle, B.R. strips down to his swim shorts, and from a ledge he dives into the flowing river wanting to see for himself if the river is as huge as reported.

As he streaks deeper, he can hardly believe what he sees. Fish usually flash a silver color, but these unclassified and breathtaking fish are gold colored with orange, red, pink, and yellow fins. The deeper he goes, the bigger the fish.

Coral was everywhere even without sunlight, and B.R. estimates he's reached one hundred feet deep with no bottom visible. It almost looks bottomless and wider than the Amazon overhead. Seeing enough by holding his breath, B.R. heads back to the surface and climbs out of the cave where he describes what he has witnessed to Bob and the guide.

"You guys will get your chance to explore the underground river once we have accomplished our mission," B.R. promised.

BACK ON TOP

Motoring on their flat bottom boat, they calculate how far down the submarine would have traveled. The plan was to determine where the sub would surface for a fresh supply of air.

Catching a couple of these smugglers, B.R. determined he could get information from them about the pink cocaine operation and where Slasher was hiding. Getting info from these guys would be hard for most anyone, but not for B.R. A ghost in the jungle could do wonders.

They settled in for a long ride down the Amazon searching for another cave opening, docking every six to eight hours to do calculations of a mini-sub underneath.

"It's not fair, these mosquitoes won't touch you, Poncho," Bob cracked to B.R.

"They don't like my blood, Cisco," he said laughing.

The flat bottom had the cabin toward the back, or stern as called on a boat, and the steering mechanism was forward of the little cabin. Inside were the hammocks and storage areas for supplies, a small table, and chairs. A grill was used for cooking inside or out and it worked with wood, especially hickory.

The little steam engine was a solid contraption that ran around ten knots per hour max. This meant there would be lots of days riding down the river.

The three boaters settled into a laid-back attitude fishing, playing cards, and generally checking out native villages and river habitat. Some natives were friendly, but others were dangerous, typical situations traveling the Amazon River.

Most of their meals were fish caught by the three, and one of their favorites was a fish named Tambaqui that eats seeds and fruit — it's considered one of the best tasting freshwater fish in the world. A member of the piranha family, the species can reach up to three feet in length and weigh up to 100 pounds. Just one of these suckers fed the three for quite a while.

Playing cards with B.R. was difficult because he could count and remember the whole deck. He had to refrain from doing it if he wanted to play.

One evening, a bad thunderstorm came out of nowhere and began rocking the boat here and there. Everyone was scurrying around with rope and canvas when a strong gust of wind literally picked up the guide and blew him overboard. By now, the whitecap waves were whipping on the river and you could barely hear the guide yelling, "Help, over here!"

This got the attention of a black caiman alligator which headed straight for him.

B.R. saw everything going on and without hesitation ran to that side of the boat yelling for Bob to get to the wheel. With a strong dive, he pitched the guide a life preserver and landed between him and alligator, which was streaking toward him with a mouth full of teeth showing above the white capped waves. The caiman's jaws and B.R.'s hands clashed at the same moment, each pushing with tremendous power to get the upper hand of attack, spinning over and around each go. When they appeared back on the surface, B.R. had maneuvered on top of the river monster, riding it like a horse.

The giant gator keeps rolling and thrashing in the waves trying to get B.R. off, twisting its head back and forth, snapping powerful jaws at him making the river look like a typhoon was rocking the river. B.R.'s legs were locked around the alligator, and he laughed as he enjoyed the ride.

"If only my old buddies in the Turkey Dolls street gang back home could see me now!" B.R. yells.

With that said, he grabs the caimans snapping jaws and with a powerful jerk snaps the creature's jaws completely apart, then throws the two jaws downstream to draw the gathering piranha away. Kicking the remaining body of the alligator away, B.R. swims swiftly to the guide and heads to the boat.

The storm is raging, and Bob is fighting the wind steering the boat back and forth away from the banks.

B.R. shouts, "You got it bro, keep her steady!" as he watches the piranha devour the alligator.

"Thank you very much," says the guide.

As the days pass by, a lot of analyzing of the underground river and its openings is done by the boaters. Searching the river's banks, they find quite a few cave-like openings but none to the river below.

They encounter all kinds of strange animals, reptiles and insects.

AMAZON HEADHUNTERS

One evening, Bob and their guide were off searching the jungle area on the river's banks for logs to drive the steam engine. The sun was sinking low, which concerned B.R. a little. They had never meandered around the jungle this time of day, considering danger was behind every tree. Bob was a well-trained lawman, but in this part of the world the unforeseen was prevalent and plentiful.

Right before dark, B.R. saw something he hadn't noticed earlier — a shrunken head on a stick back in the jungle trees. This usually meant "STAY AWAY" to anyone that decided to enter their territory.

"This ain't good," B.R. said to himself.

B.R. was a super fighter and he instinctively sprang into action. Out came the Black Recluse uniform and motorcycle. Docking the boat close to shore, B.R. revs the Harley engine with the silent muffler and jumps the span of water to the bank. Off into the jungle he goes, zig-zagging trees and undergrowth, sometimes leaping logs and obstacles and going airborne from mounds and such.

He covers about five square miles in less than a few minutes, while all the time slinging snakes and sharp-toothed monkeys off that jump him as he passes through the bushes.

Finally, he sees a light from a campfire up ahead. Slowing down to a crawl, the Recluse maneuvers his bike to the edge of a native village. Just as he had expected, Bob and the guide are sitting in a bamboo cage. They had fallen into a hidden trap set by the native headhunters and was awaiting the ritual of shrinking their heads to begin. The guide was petrified, but Bob was calm knowing the Recluse very well and had confidence he would figure things out. Action was just a moment away.

The Black Recluse saw the situation and decided on the plan of action. He determined there would be no killing. After all, they were in the headhunter's territory and the three agents were the ones invading their space. It would be tricky, the Recluse thought to himself.

He finds a good size limb for a club, and the "ghost" Recluse would hopefully scare the natives. Ready for a strike, he turns full ghost lights on and hits the throttle. Doing a wheelie, he jets toward the unsuspecting natives and with an eerie ghost-like laugh, he is a scary sight to behold.

When the village of headhunters sees the Black Recluse heading straight for them, they holler and scream as if they are seeing a real ghost. That's exactly what the Recluse was betting on.

The natives scatter in every direction, so the Recluse pulls his shotgun and blows out a side of the bamboo cage.

"Run like the wind," he orders.

Off in the direction of the boat the two hostages flee. Bob had carefully remembered the direction of the way the natives had brought them with spears sticking in their backs.

The native chief gathers his panic and orders the others to stop running.

"Attack this intruder," he commands in his native language. Ghost or not, he had decided to fight.

The Recluse turns and sees them coming, and arrows with poison tips begin filling the air. The bulletproof suit will stop the arrows, and he heads straight for them with his club.

"Got to teach these guys some manners," laughs the Black Recluse.

With club swinging and bike motoring, he knocks one after another to the ground. The natives try to grab hold of him, but the Recluse is way too strong and fast for that. Riding in a circle, he brings most of them to the ground with his club.

"There's going to be some serious headaches after this," the Recluse laughs.

Motoring to a grove of trees, he turns his lights off and seems to disappear. This really freaks the headhunters out and they yell to one another, "He really is a ghost!"

The Recluse figures the other two have had enough time to make it close to the boat, so off he heads to join them.

Once on board, they steam off down the river.

"Man was I glad to see you. The ghost effect did the trick," Bob said.

"Yeah, and if it hadn't worked, a lot of blood would have spilled getting you two out of that cage," says the Recluse.

HOSTAGES

Two weeks pass searching the Amazon banks for one of the hidden entrances down to the Rio Hamza River that B.R. has calculated. The river runner's spirits are still high because they are simply enjoying the exploration of this amazing part of the world.

"We need to make some progress on this project before too long. The home office back in Nashville is getting a little antsy," Bob explains in a "Cheech" voice imitation that he often does.

"I know what you're trying to pull. You would like me to imitate Chong," laughs B.R.

"I think we should find a cave about anytime," says the guide.

The next day, it rains so hard they decide to kick back and wait for the hot sun to dry things out. Playing cards and grilling canned hamburgers are on tap to pass away this kind of day.

Eight o'clock next morning, Bob wakes the other two and tells them it has stopped raining, so they need to get moving. Off they go looking for a hole in the ground with their fingers crossed. Swinging his machete, B.R. whacks bushes so they can squeeze through the undergrowth when suddenly he says, "Stop."

His super hearing detects the faint sound of bats which means there probably is a cave entrance close by. As they scan the area, they finally find exactly what they were searching for — a hidden cave entrance.

Bulldog bats with wing spans of two feet had just settled down for the day after a night of catching fish and scorpions.

They could be heard down inside hanging from the cave ceiling.

"Bats give me the creeps," Bob said.

"Well at least they ain't vampire bats that would suck your blood. You do know those bats live in South America?" the guide quipped.

One by one, they lowered themselves down to the cave floor. With flashlights and lanterns, they could tell this was one of the main supply stops for the drug runners. Dry foods, water, and barrels of diesel fuel were stacked in a corner.

"Looks as though no one has stopped because nothing has been opened. This is good because I have a plan," B.R. explains.

He lays out his plan to Bob and the guide. Everyone will take turns hiding out and waiting for two men and the sub. B. R. analyzes that it will not be long to wait. When the water in the underground river starts bubbling, that means the submarine is surfacing. Whoever is on guard duty will shine a flashlight up through the cave opening, and the other two will go into action. B.R. will dress in his Black Recluse suit, and Bob will get ready to take a long ride in a submarine.

Two days pass and B.R. is on guard duty. Suddenly he sees bubbles floating to the surface. Shining his light upwards, the other two hurry down from their little camp site.

Everyone hides behind cave walls and waits to see what is fixing to go down. The top of the small sub comes into view from the deep. It churns close to the bank, and a door winds around until it springs open. One smuggler pops out taking in the fresh cave air, then wades to the bank. The other submariner follows, and they start jabbering in their native language.

The guide speaks their language and whispers to B.R. what they are saying. As they see the stack of supplies, one rubs his belly and laughs, "Hungry."

Out of the dark, the Black Recluse taps both on the shoulder and freaked, they spring around, staring down the barrels of a 12 gauge.

"Remind them that this OO buckshot will cut them in half," B.R. tells the guide.

They wisely don't put up a fight.

With hands tied sitting on the ground, they listen to the guide explain what's in store for the two mules. The Recluse knows they will have to communicate with the drug lord by radio, and after he finds out which one drives the sub, he tells him that Agent Jarvis is riding with him to his next supply stop.

The other is going top side and will be spilling his guts about this operation.

"No way can they get anything from me," the smuggler thinks to himself.

Back on the boat the Black Recluse grabs the Smuggler's arm and with a razor-sharp knife cuts an Indian "blood brother" gash across his hand.

He looks at the Recluse and grins.

"That's all you got?" he says after spitting in the face of the FBI's top gun.

Very soon, the drug man finds himself hanging upside down from a tree limb inches from the river water. Both hands and feet are tied and the blood from his hand is dripping into the water. He pulls his head and shoulders up by his legs to stay away from the water, but he can only hold himself up for so long. Eventually, his head drops inches from the water, and the piranha are in a frenzy leaping up and taking nibbles of flesh from his face and shoulders.

The Recluse lights a strand of the rope holding the wiggling captive to the limb. The flame starts burning slowly up to the knot holding him. Now, the smuggler is feeling like talking.

The Recluse tells the sub driver that if he doesn't get a clear message to the Slasher, the two will be nothing but bones.

"This is what you will say and do. Call your boss and tell him a new drug lord is taking over this territory and the pink cocaine empire. If the Slasher wants to work for me, we can get together at the next supply stop of his mules' submarine run," the Recluse orders.

He knows the kingpin will be in a rage and come to kill this threat, and that's just what the Black Recluse wants.

By now the flame has gotten closer to the rope knot, and the captive is screaming and begging for his life as the piranha are doing a number on his flesh, even hanging out of the water.

Both coke runners are yelling they'll do whatever the Recluse wants.

"Please get me down while I've still got some hide left on my head!" the captive screams.

"If I were you, I'd think twice before I spit in someone's face," the Recluse tells the guide to interpret. He then tells Bob to get him down.

The two men agree to do what the Recluse wants as they doctor up the captive with piranha bites.

The sub driver says, "We have heard of the Black Recluse and the passion to catch people like us. Are you human or something else?"

"I wouldn't worry too much about what you've heard. You better be thinking about what will happen to you if you double cross me. We might give you a break if you play the game," the Recluse said.

Bob and the sub driver load supplies and are submerged in the underground river. The call is made to Sergio Slasher Mendez and the plan is set in motion.

"I'm going to kill me a cocaine intruder!" Sergio screams when he hears the threat of someone trying to take his territory.

Bob is inquisitive about this small underwater machine made by Germans. He also has a 45-caliber pistol sticking in the sub driver's ear.

"Hey dude, just do as you were told," Bob tells him, knowing he doesn't speak English, but also knowing he understands "gun."

THE RENDEZVOUS

The Recluse changes outfits and has the boat wheel headed downstream to the next sub stop disclosed by the captive who was placed at the bow of the flatboat leading them to the destination.

B.R. and the guide discuss what they are going to do when the Slasher arrives at the destination.

"I've got this old steamer running as fast as it will go, and we've got to get there first to succeed on this mission. Then again, it doesn't matter who gets there first. I'm so ready for this takedown because I was born to be wild," B.R. says to the guide, loving the adventure.

It takes over a week to reach the next cave opening, but with the cocaine smuggler explaining where to look, it makes it a whole lot quicker. They check to see if they arrived before the submarine. Sure enough, they beat the underwater boat to the supply cave and a sigh of relief comes from the two boaters.

B.R. and the guide jump into arranging booby traps. They find a low spot in the area of the cave, so they stretch a large fishing net across it. Securing it with wooden stakes then covering it with jungle underbrush makes it completely hidden from anyone that doesn't know it's been set.

Then they make two rope springs that, once stepped on, will jerk a man high into the tree by their foot leaving him dangling upside down.

They tie the drug runner to a tree on the path leading to the cave as a decoy for ole Slasher who is traveling to this location in a jeep and a large military style truck full of his ruthless entourage. Sergio is so insane from anger he is falling for this trap like a moth to a flame as B.R. knew he would.

"What a moron," he laughs.

The Black Recluse suit is hanging nearby but out of sight and ready to be worn in action.

"I'll be in my fighting clothes like a flash of lightning. I've got the jerk that's tied to the tree so confused he has no clue who's who," B.R. smirks to the guide.

Around dusk, the familiar sound of bubbles are heard by the powerful ear of B.R.

"I bet that crazy agent Jarvis is ready to get out of that sub just to get away from the smell of that driver's armpits," B.R. chuckles. The guide says nothing but grins for the first time in a while.

Bob and the sub driver appear from the cave to be met by the glowing ghost of the Black Recluse.

"When is the Slasher arriving?" he asked in that creepy electronic voice. The driver estimated it should be sometime between midnight and dawn.

"Well I see my comrade is tied up, and those scabs on his face are going to piss the Slasher off," growled the sub man.

The Recluse sticks the barrels of his shotgun in his mouth and says, "One more word out of you punk, and oops, a spider has got your tongue."

Sweat pours down the freaked out man's face.

Midnight finds the jungle lightly visible in a crescent moon giving the mist an aura and eerie-like effect. Somewhere plowing through the massive botanical lungs of the earth, the engines of a jeep and trucks are straining toward the supply cave. The Recluse hears the faint sounds of the engines and tells everyone to take the positions of attack as planned.

One drug hostage is tied directly across from the hidden low area, and the other is sitting by a campfire approximately 300 hundred feet to the left. Agent Jarvis is hidden well behind the area packing a Thompson machine gun. The Recluse is across from him sitting on his bike with shotgun in hand completely blended in the jungle darkness and breathing heavily with adrenaline and venom flowing overtime in his veins.

As the headlights appear from out of the undergrowth, Sergio Slasher Mendez has his driver turn toward the right because he catches a glimpse of his mule tied to a tree and still does not rationalize that he has been manipulated by the Recluse into this trap. He feels invincible to any threat — after all, he has exterminated military and law enforcement by the dozens in and around Northern parts of South America. Problem — the Black Recluse is a whole different ballgame.

The Slasher and three gunmen leap out of the jeep and go to his drug runner sitting by the campfire and angrily ask him, "What in hell's name are you doing just sitting here , and where is this slime that thinks he can take my territory?"

The mule whispers in a scared and shaky voice, "The Black Recluse," looking around the jungle.

"You mean to tell me that you went along with this aberration of an FBI agent?" Slasher asked.

In a fit of rage, he pulls his gun and puts a bullet right between his eyes. At that moment, the truck full of killers drive toward the tied captive and BLAM! — nose down goes the truck into the covered low area. It slams so hard in the ground the driver is thrown through the windshield, ripping his testicles off on the steering wheel and pushing his jaw bones into his skull. Two other men riding shotgun are thrown through the windshield getting slashed from head to toe from the glass as they go through. The riders in back are slung every which way and scramble to regain their weapons because they know it's a trap.

The Slasher runs toward them and "oops" — he steps in a tree spring that jerks him fifty feet in the air by his ankle. He starts firing his assault rifle in every direction of the jungle's edge.

"I'll make monkey meat out of you, Spider!" he screams. His fighters regroup and begin firing with rifles and machine guns. They don't know who or where their adversaries are hidden, but they know they are fixing to attack. The jungle is about to erupt in an all-out jungle war.

As the Slasher yells, "Kill them!" from his upside-down hanging position, the guide flips on a high-powered light from a strategically hidden position in a cluster of trees. He shines it back and forth right in the small army's eyes, momentarily blinding them. That's when they hear the ghostly voice of the Black Recluse's laughter. Out of the dark with all lights on, he jets straight toward the disoriented drug cartel warriors who begin firing blindly in every direction. That's when Agent Jarvis opens up with his machine gun, forcing the group to find cover and return fire.

The Recluse is now on top of them, and all lights go out, but the spider's vision penetrates the dark and his twelve gauge drops two in an instant. He feels the hot sting of bullets hitting his specially made suit, but it only infuriates him that much more. In an instant, he reloads while leaning and turning his bike in a circle for more targets to take out.

Meanwhile, the Slasher is trying to climb up the rope to the limb that holds him.

"If I can get out of this tree, I'm putting a bullet between that creature's ears," he yells.

By now bullets are flying everywhere. Some find their target but most miss because the Black Recluse is a blur on his cycle. He takes two more down and Bob takes out three. The killers realize they are in an ambush position, so they split up and try looping back around to get in a better firing position.

One cartel fighter works his way around agent Jarvis and opens fire. They battle each other a few minutes, and Bob feels a burning pain in his upper chest as a bullet goes through him. He yells at the Recluse to let him know he's wounded.

The guide flips on the spotlight again, and the Recluse goes flying through the gunshots dropping one fighter after another with his 45-caliber pistol, ignoring the pain from bullets bouncing off his suit.

"You can't kill a ghost,!" he screams.

This starts freaking the killers out, and they don't know whether to shoot or run.

By then, the Recluse has eliminated five more in a blazing gun fight. Three cartel fighters decide to flee and run through the jungle's edge trying to escape this fighting machine they have encountered.

After taking down eight more of Slasher's army, the remaining surrender by throwing their weapons out toward the campfire.

The Recluse says, "Don't try to fool me. Come out by the firelight and lay down or I'll blow your brains out."

Apparently, some speak English and with that, the remaining fighters lay down by the fire.

"Tie them up," he tells the guide while he checks on Bob, who tells the Recluse he was wearing a bulletproof vest that was sleeveless, but a bullet struck his upper chest and shoulder that was barely exposed.

"Man, the pain is unbelievable," he moans.

"Let me get the first aid kit and some morphine," says the Recluse.

Suddenly, the area is sprayed with rifle bullets. Up in the tree, the Slasher had worked his way down to a limb thirty feet from the ground.

"You'll pay for this if it's the last thing I do!" shouts Sergio.

"Well you just jump on down and I'll catch you, Mr. Mendez," the Recluse hollers out.

"Oh, I'm coming down, you snake!" Slasher yells.

The Recluse tells his guide to hand him Bob's machine gun and proceeds to riddle the limb holding Sergio, who tries holding on but to no avail. The impact of the fall shatters his neck, and he knows that he is paralyzed. The thought of such a thing to live in prison with was too much. He barely can reach into his pocket to pull out a pistol and then points it at his temple and fires. The notorious pink cocaine cartel is no more.

"All I can say is this takedown was simply too easy, all because the Slasher's temper blinded his plan of retaliation. How stupid and no common sense," the Black Recluse states.

Wrapping things up with the captive cartel army and the complete operation, B.R. has Bob Jarvis airlifted by helicopter to a hospital in Bogota, Colombia where he is hospitalized to heal. FBI agents move in and shut down what remains of this incredible pink cocaine operation.

B.R. takes a jet back to Nashville and tells Chief L.J. of what an incredible adventure of education and danger it has been in a part of the earth that has so much to do with the planet's lifeline.

DO YOU BELIEVE IN WEREWOLVES

L.J. tells B.R. to rest up for a couple of days and maybe go out on the town for a little fun, then the chief looks B.R. in the eye and with a very serious tone of voice says, "We all are going to have a meeting Monday morning. I've been corresponding with J. Edgar Hoover and he tells me something strange and sinister is sweeping the mountains and towns East of Los Angeles."

B.R. stares back at him with those piercing brown eyes and picks up the conversation.

"The wolf 'thing' is what you're suggesting, isn't it?"

Then L.J. asked, "Do you believe in werewolves, spider man?"

Pausing for a moment before answering the chief's question, B.R. states, "I have heard about such a creature all my life, but I have never seen one or a real ghost for that matter."

The next Monday, Chief L.J. explains to B.R. and agents their next assignment, and it's a doozy. He tells them to research anything and everything about the subject of wolf creatures.

"Leave nothing unturned," he said, giving them a week to cram as much information and folklore on the subject as they can.

"You got it, boss, with extreme doubts of finding anything real about this kind of hogwash. I'm thinking it won't be long before I'll be facing aliens," B.R. chuckles.

The more he delves into lycanthropy, the more B.R. thinks to himself, "This is all a bunch of folklore and myths. There ain't no such thing as a werewolf. Some idiot might think he is one, but pretending is about all it can amount to. I don't know where J. Edgar is getting his info, but I think my boss L.J. is only trying to appease him to keep down contradictions and embarrassments. I might as well play along, and it may take more than a week or two for this kind of research."

And then, it begins.......

LYCANTHROPY

In folklore, a werewolf or occasionally lycanthrope is a human with the ability to shapeshift into a wolf, either purposely or after being placed under a curse or affliction.

Mythological origin — Europe. Abilities: Superhuman speed, superhuman endurance, healing factor, superhuman senses, agility, vision, and strength.

Superhuman agility. A werewolf's agility, balance, and bodily coordination are enhanced to levels

146

that are beyond the natural physical limits of even the finest human athlete. They can move, jump, climb, and run incredibly fast without difficulty or exhaustion.

One of the most powerful, addictive reasons humans were drawn to becoming a werewolf was the elevated pleasure of sexual (breeding) copulation which would last for hours or days with a male and female werewolf or a werewolf and a human. Females are referred to as a were woman.

Lycanthrope — Origin Greek-wolf man. History: Catherine Clark Kroeger has written that several parts of the Bible refer to King Nebuchadnezzar's behavior in the book of Daniel 4 as a being manifestation of clinical lycanthropy.

Neurologist Andrew J. Larner has written that the fate of Odysseus's crew due to the magic of Circe may be one of the earliest examples of clinical lycanthropy. Also, it is believed that the King of Armenia Tridates III also suffered from this disorder. He was cured by Gregory the Illuminator. As a sign of gratitude, Tridates proclaimed Christianity as the state religion during 301, thus making Armenia the first Christian state.

According to Persian tradition, the Buyid Prince Majd Oldudawla was suffering from an illusion that he was a cow. He was cured by Avicenna.

Notions that Lycanthropy was due to a medical condition go back to the seventh century when the Alexandrian physician Paulus Aegineta attributed lycanthropy to melancholia or an "excess of black bile." During 1563, a Lutheran physician named Johann

Weyer wrote that werewolves suffered from an imbalance in their melancholic humor and exhibited the physical symptoms of paleness — "a dry tongue and a great thirst" — as well as sunken, dim, and dry eyes. Even King James VI and I in his 1597 Treatise Daemonologie does not blame werewolf behavior on delusions created by the Devil but "an excess of melancholy as the culprit which causes some men to believe that they are wolves and to 'counterfeit' the actions of these animals."

The perception of an animalistic behavior can be traced throughout the history of folklore from many different countries. Symptoms: Affected individuals believe that they are in the process of transforming into an animal or have already transformed into an animal. It has been associated with the altered states of mind that accompanies psychosis (the mental state that typically involves delusions and hallucinations) with the transformation only seeming to happen in the mind and behavior of the affected person.

From the Mclean Hospital, a patient reports in a moment of lucidity or reminiscence that they sometimes feel as an animal or have felt like one.

A patient behaves in a manner that resembles animal behavior, for example howling, growling, or crawling.

According to criteria, either a delusional belief in current or past transformation or behavior that suggests a person thinks of themselves as transformed is considered evidence of clinical lycanthropy. The authors note that although the condition seems to be an expression of psychosis, there is no specific diagnosis of mental or neurological illness associated with its behavioral consequences. One important factor may be differences or changes in parts of the brain known to be involved in representing body shape. (Proprioception and body image).

A neuroimaging study of two people diagnosed with clinical lycanthropy showed that these areas display unusual activity, suggesting that when people report that their bodies are changing shape, they may be genuinely perceiving those feelings.

It has been described as "the sense of being in the wrong (species) body — A desire to be an animal."

The phenomenon is also a powerful subliminal, biokinesis binaural beat hypnosis meditation spell.

The power of the mind is much more powerful than you can ever imagine. The mind has the power to change physical aspects such as color of eyes, hair color, and shape or growth.

After studying this and more, B.R. believes that you've got to be out of your mind for such bull crap.

"Maybe I need to purchase some silver bullets," he laughs out loud.

LOS ANGELES

Northeast of Los Angeles is the San Gabriel Mountains, the San Gabriel Valley, and after that is the Mojave Desert.

A man lives alone on the outskirts of this City of Angels, called this because Los Angeles means The Angels in Spanish. He had traveled here from Romania and became a United States citizen in 1948. Alexandru Nicolae graduated from Oxford in England with top honors. He was a brilliant mind, and spoke four languages fluently — Romanian, Russian, Spanish, and English.

Alexandru never married but lived as a playboy, and he could charm the ladies, which was one reason he came to L.A. with its Hollywood atmosphere and beautiful women. Because of these gorgeous girls, Alexandru slowly started contemplating one of the most bizarre schemes ever concocted by man.

Somewhere, maybe in his hometown, he had read where a werewolf could mate for hours or days, and that set plans in motion of a sinister plan to learn all about Lycanthropy.

Researching everything he could find about this subject for almost a year, he started putting his "dream" plan together. Alexandru had to know if werewolves were a myth or was it true.

Deciding it might be induced for a human to transform, he turned to chemistry. Being very scientifically minded, he created a laboratory in a back room of his house. Mixing various organic herbs with chemical compounds, he was deep into this project. Thinking about the power and agility of a werewolf captured his every thought.

Then he jumped into hypnotism and became a seasoned mind controlling manipulator. He was cruising along at light speed to become a wolf creature, and the thought of also creating a wolfwoman sent shock waves through his warped brain.

Even though he experimented feverishly for months, his patience began paying off, finally. He was a wealthy man from inheritance, so now it was the only thing he wanted to do, even slowing down his playboy lifestyle.

Would he find a potion which could change him permanently or just for a day? He was determined to find the answer. After trying different combinations, he finally hit on one that enhanced his body hair to lengthen ever so slightly. He knew he was on to something that seemed promising.

Experimenting for another month, it became clear which combination it took to transform him. He had found a potion that really changed a human into a wolf-like creature. It didn't extend his face or give him fangs, but the hair on his entire body grew long like a wolf and it was snow white, a haunting sight for sure.

It gave him all the abilities of the wolf — strength, vision, agility, endurance, and speed. He designed a set of fangs for his mouth and claws for his hands and feet. Alexandru was a wolf creature!

The potion would last approximately twenty-four

hours each time he would down a vale of his creation which contained blood from a wolf. Apparently, this was why he started craving flesh to eat from an animal when he was transformed into a wolf creature.

The question that drove him to this insane state was the sexual part of being a wolf creature, and he was literally dying to find out. This fantasy would lead him to a horrendously evil plan that would plague Southern California for a long, long time.

THE SAN GABRIEL PLAGUE

Right around this time, J.R. was on the Knoxville Police Force making a name for himself. Alexandru and his destiny were on a collision course somewhere in the future because the wolf creature ravaged the San Gabriel Valley for a very long time.

Alexandru begins a search for a remote spot in the San Gabriel Valley to complete his iniquitous nightmare. He studies the valley and mountains for a perfect hideaway. Searching through maps and books on the area, he finds a place that might just be perfect for his ideals.

On the foothills of the San Gabriel mountain range was an old mine shaft that had been deserted for years, and it rested on the back side of a small mountain obscure from the valley about twenty miles away. It also had a shack on the property that Alexandru thought could be enlarged and made livable. Not being in the national park, he set out to find the owner, and eventually he did.

The mining company still owned the property, so Alexandru disguised himself and with a false name and identification bought the acreage explaining he was considering opening a tourist attraction if the county would build a good highway up to it. He knew this county would never spend that kind of money so these were all lies to make sure everyone would eventually forget all about the place, and they did. The plan had evolved like a lucky charm.

The valley to L.A. was only 18 miles apart, so Alexandru decided to keep his operating lab in his Los Angeles house.

He bought a camper and pulled it up to the mineshaft to design a commune type quarters to hide away in. First, the shack was enlarged two stories, but with old material to look as though it hadn't been used. Then he designs and builds living cells in the mine, having to reinforce the walls and ceilings. He accomplishes this trick by hiring migrant workers from Wyoming and hauling material at night. Luck was on his side because nobody ever had a clue. Alexandru paid the workers a lot of money and told them to keep quiet so he could surprise the community with his tourist attractions on opening day.

While the mineshaft was being worked on, Alexandru decided to purchase a house in Arcadia that was in the valley and close to the mountains. He was getting weary of the camper life and wanted to try a night with his potion.

It didn't have to be a full moon to transform, but when he did without clothes on and white hair covering his body, the full moon shining on him was outrageously scary. It was something never seen on this earth — maybe on a planet far, far away!

One night he drank a shot glass of potion he brought back from L.A., and when it hits his veins, Alexandru rips his clothes off and out the back door he dashes into the dark, moonless night. Swiftly he goes through neighborhoods until he smells the scent of an animal. The adrenaline was pumping overtime, and as he quickly circles a house, he sees a large dog lying next to its doghouse. Before the poor animal can growl, the wolf creature's fangs are around its throat, ripping it apart.

After viciously eating a large portion of the dog's frame, he rushes off to the outskirts of town and hides the remains, never to be found.

With an eerie howl, he disappears again back into the darkness of night. When he reaches his house, the wolf creature sits in a chair staring straight ahead with ecstasy filling his brain, not moving a muscle until the potion wears off. Alexandru didn't want anything to distract this feeling deep inside him because he was now totally consumed.

The mine is finished with cell pods deep inside the shaft tunnel, and each is furnished like a luxury kitchenette that stays around 65 to 70 degrees year round.

The shack is lavishly furnished with a huge basement four times as large as the shack's square footage. Everything to live in total comfort is sneaked in, and the next step in Alexandru's diabolical plan is in the works.

On the backstreets of Los Angeles he researches for the names of anyone who is involved with human trafficking, particularly young teenage girls and boys with a few young women and men. His plan is to colonize a wolfman and woman cult following.

He then contacts drug dealers for narcotics to use himself and for his soon-to-be followers that he will get addicted to them as well. Alexandru wants to experience the "high" of both himself and the changeling wolf creature at the same time. A deadly storm is approaching the valley.

THE COLONIZATION

Alexandru connects with a treacherous Argentine man who is someone that can get you most anything for a price. This was no problem for the wealthy Romanian.

"I need humans," Alexandru explains.

"No problem," Argentine man says.

"I'll need more than one truck load," Alexandru excitedly states.

"I will bring the truck load to Los Angeles, and then it's all yours," the thug explains.

After all the arrangements are made, Alexandru vanishes to the mine shack and with narcotics getting him stoned, he downs another vial of his potion with a full moon rising. With the drugs and potion kicking, he walks out into the light of the moon and howls uncontrollably, reveling in this super rush.

Suddenly, he sprints up the side of the mountain, jumping rocks and crevices like the wind itself. Smelling blood, his eyes glow red as he sees a mountain goat on a cliff. Zeroing in on his prey, his white hair in the moonlight is like a trace of light streaking upside the mountain. What a creepy, evil aberration it makes.

Soon the goat flees but the wolf creature is hot on its scent and trail. Within a minute, the mountain goat that ordinarily could out jump most predators on the side of a mountain is slashed with claws that disable it quickly. With blood pouring from the goat, the wolfman chews flesh and bone until satisfied. Seems nothing can defend against this monster. The howling goes on till the wee hours of morning.

This is all happening while J.R. Dawkins is becoming the top ace for the FBI back in Nashville, Tennessee. Make no mistake, the paths of J.R. Dawkins aka The Black Recluse and Alexandru Nicolae aka the Wolf Creature will cross sometime in the future. The first truck full of bought human captives are delivered secretly to L.A. and then taken to the mine in the San Gabriel mountains. Eight teens and six young adults are led into the mine cells. Each one is assigned a separate pod, and even though they are petrified of not knowing what they are fixing to face, the fact they have a new clean apartment is a long way up from what they have been through most of their lives. They were used as sex slaves, forced to be subjected to all kinds of psychos.

Unable to escape because of leg chains, and with Alexandru wielding a machine gun and keeping them drugged, their will to flee was almost zero. Keeping them addicted to heroin was a priority, but Alexandru wanted them to be more alert so the dosage was slowly lightened.

They were fed nutritional meals and were required to exercise to improve their deteriorated physical conditions. Alexandru was their psychologist and worked with them on mental issues, and then he started hypnotic suggestions to draw them to himself as if he was their savior.

Hypnosis and heroin can make anyone do anything, period. Alexandru's goal is to develop sex slave wolf people at his disposal. The plan is to get this first truck load developed and colonized, then bring another truck full in and repeat the process, which would be like creating a harem of young girls and women. He didn't care how young or what nationality they were.

One thing that was so crazy about his chemical drink was that no matter what hair color a person had, it would turn pure white while under its spell. They could continue the transformation just by drinking one after another.

No one in this day and time would ever believe in such a thing as a werewolf. This made it much easier for Alexandru to accomplish his unimaginable project. Even though the claws and fangs were man made, they were razor sharp and deadly.

Alexandru decided he needed a female partner for himself, and two males to help keep law and order among the colony. Someone he could trust by using extra hypnotic suggestions. He picked a young adult female that in his eyes was the best looking. She would be his do-all in every way and be by his side as he roamed the night searching for prey. This young lady he named Dawn.

The two males were young adults and were the most muscular of the colony. They were to always stay near Alexandru and protect. He named them Moon and Sky.

It was getting time to introduce his wolf potion to the three picks. This would be the first humans besides Alexandru to experience this satanic man-made lycanthropy. The vials were locked and hidden in the shack basement.

Alexandru decided to wait for a full moon to give them the full effect of being a wolf creature. Moonlit white hair streaking on the hunt. He was so vainly proud of his accomplishment.

He had moved Dawn into the shack with him but was having sex with all the girls. The thought of breeding as animals was about to explode his evil brain. The dream he had concocted was soon to be a reality.

THE WOLF CREATURE SCOURGE

A full moon big as a whale was creeping up the Eastern horizon and excitement was at a fever pitch in the mine colony, especially in Alexandru. The time to go on the hunt was here, so he ordered his three picks to take off their clothes and drink his potion. Apprehensively they followed his lead. When the vial of serum hit their bloodstream, the transformation quickly began. Each received a set of fangs and claws, and Alexandru led Dawn, Moon, and Sky out of the shack into the bright, moon shadowy night. Seeing the glow of their white furry hair was beautiful to him. With patches of fog here and there, the landscape was evilly ghost-like, like from another planet.

Over the rocks and bushes they swiftly glided like a cold wind. They all felt a sense of animalistic freedom as if flying across the earth's surface, a feeling never before felt by a human. How could anything of this magnitude be happening, and was this something from the dark pits of the underground driving chosen followers?

As the smell of prey penetrated their animalistic brains, they branched off in separate directions after a hunt. Moon was chasing a jack rabbit which he quickly caught and bit in half. Sky was on the scent of a grey Zorro (fox), and he also crushed the animal.

Alexandru and Dawn picked up a strong smell of a cat, and a big cat for sure. They came across the den of a mountain lion, so here was the first test of being a Lobo creature, and how would they fare? As they approached the lion, each went in a circle to move in for the kill. Being high on a rock ledge and standing its ground, the lion lets out an intimidating growl with eyes like steel. The wolf man and woman jet so fast and cunning, the cat is attacked from both sides. The huge lion fiercely slashes and bites in defense, only to be surprisingly taken down and ripped to death. It was absolutely no match for a wolf creature's strength and speed, let alone two lobo creatures.

Instantly, Alexandru dives in, eating flesh and fur with blood running off his chin. Dawn tries a bite or two but slowly backs away to Alexandrus surprise. He later finds out that Sky and Moon don't devour their kill either. Something isn't adding up with his calculations when creating his chemical and wolf blood potion.

Back at the compound in his hideaway, Alexandru contemplates a couple of things he considers extremely important. One thing he wants is to develop the skill of running on all fours like the wolf. He decides with patience it could be accomplished, then hypnotically suggested it to the colony. The other concerning illogic of being a true werewolf is the craving for raw flesh.

He digs into human behavior with books he collects from a library. His conclusion is the people he bought were mentally and physically tortured, which made them withdrawn and compassionate about life. In other words, no amount of hypnotic suggestions could break through their subliminal thought process. They were not the exact vicious type of people to be true wolf people. That's why they didn't have the craving to eat raw flesh.

After sleeping on these findings, Alexandru decided what he needed was a person or persons that were natural born killers. He knew this would be risky in every way, but he had come too far to turn back now even if it risked his own life. Being able to have complete control of a person like that was his challenge.

Back in L.A., the search was on for a certain kind of human being of this nature, maybe two or even three? Killers or torturers was the word out on the backstreets, and after a few days Alexandru got a call from a man who addressed himself as the Arranger. Alexandru had a scrambler on his phone so nobody could recognize his voice. He explained to the Arranger what his needs were, and that was three men as bodyguards to protect his home since he traveled a lot, so they had to be tough. The home address Alexandru used was nonexistent, and he left nothing for chance. The Arranger told him to allow a couple of days for the time it would take, so this gave Alexandru time to go back to the colony and check with Moon and Sky whom he had left in charge. Everything was fine, and he missed Dawn, which was something new for him since he never fell for any woman, but this new style of living made him feel different. Dawn was a beautiful woman now that she had her health back.

Very soon the Arranger got word to Alexandru he had three men that fit his needs very well. One from Russia and two from the African country of Uganda. All three could speak broken English, and they were exactly what he wanted — three cut throats! They were to be picked up in Los Angeles in two days, and they came with a very high price to work for Alexandru.

During this time, he had mixed a combination of marijuana, heroin, and quaaludes, which is methaqualone, a sedative and hypnotic medication. By combining the three together, he could administer it to a Nile River crocodile and control the largest freshwater predator in Africa.

When Alexandru, Moon, and Sky picked up the three new members, they offered them a stiff shot of Jack Daniels which is a favorite worldwide, although hard to get outside the USA.

"Yes sir," growled one of the Africans, and all three downed the Tennessee whiskey in one gulp. Unknowingly, the whiskey was laced with the three "downers" Alexandru had formulated. Within a few minutes the born killers were "stoned" out of their mind and completely docile.

Once they all arrived at the compound, Alexandru put the three in a hypnotic and deep trance for complete control of their actions. He wanted undaunting loyalty from them, so with a daily dose of these sedatives and hypnotic commands, he had the three under complete control. What he really wanted from them was the killer aggressiveness when changed into a wolf creature. Oh my, Alexandru was so proud of his demonic self.

Finally, Alexandru was satisfied he had placed every piece of his puzzle together. After a couple of hypnotic sessions with everyone in the compound about running on all fours, he said it's time for everyone to experience the thrill of the hunt.

After vials of potion are swallowed, off into the night all eighteen from the colony scatter through the mountains in search of prey. The feeling of practically flying over the harsh terrain was breathtaking to the changelings. The two Africans with black skin made their white hair stand out even more. Everyone had mastered running on hands and feet.

As the sun approaches, Alexandru is first back at the shack watching who had eaten their kill. Just as he had suspected, only the three bad boys had blood splattered on their white bodies.

Dawn sensed what Alexandru was looking for, and leaned ever so close to him and said, "I'm sorry."

He was satisfied, though, because the rough guys came through for what he wanted and he had already settled on the rest for sexual purposes.

He and Dawn had already proven what he had heard about a long time ago, and that was a werewolf and were-woman could copulate for twenty-four hours or more nonstop. Alexandru had found his ultimate accomplishment, and he was addicted. His sick desires were even done with the young teenagers. He as a wolf creature and the girls without the potion. They, being completely under his trance could only do his bidding. There is a special place in Hell for a person so evil. Even with these satanic emotions controlling his mind, there was something brewing in his brain far worse than his lust he had for women!

THINGS GO DEADLY

Alexandru bought five more colonist from human traffickers, and they were converted the same as the others, which made a total of twenty three. The hills were full of streaking white-haired wolf creatures, and all native animals were in danger of being wiped out. Surprisingly, this had gone completely unnoticed by the surrounding population because Alexandru was an expert and a cunning son-of-a-gun!

Things started to ever-so-slightly change in Alexandru. He had been drinking his concoction for a long time, and it was beginning to make him feel like he needed more from his transformation as a wolf creature. Maybe his brain was being eaten away cell by cell?

One morning as Alexandru awoke from a restless night, his warped brain told him to transform and go into a town instead of the mountains, which could only mean one thing and that was hunt humans as prey! Maybe deep down he knew why he needed the three born killers in his command. He had someone to help carry out the mysterious feelings he had felt in his restless nights of dreaming. Another piece of his puzzle that he hadn't foreseen in this most ungodly and sickening formulation anyone could possibly have put together. Hollywood couldn't have written such a screen play. Come Hell or high water, Alexandru was born to be a true, blue wolfman no matter whom he destroyed in the process. A bad moon rising was about to explode.

The reign of terror started one moonless night as four wolf creatures ascended on the small town in the San Gabriel Valley named Seneca, California with an Asian population. It was a quiet night, not even a breeze, and seemed most people had retired early for bed being a Sunday evening. Patches of fog were forming here and there across the valleys making it look a little spooky outside. In the distance, a radio next to someone's open window tuned to the Grand Ole Opry station was lightly heard through the neighborhood. Other than that, it was dead as a cemetery.

As the four glided on the fringes of town, they came upon a small house with only the living room light on. They could smell the human that was inside, so they circled silent as ghosts to the back porch and ran their claws down the outside kitchen wall, creating an unearthly faint sound the occupant could hear. The elderly Asian widow heard the sound but thought the wind must have picked up, not thinking more of it.

Another wolf creature knocked lightly on the back door, which by then certainly frightened the old lady, but she told herself it might be one of the local kids that played in her backyard occasionally. Hearing the knock again, she crosses the kitchen floor and flips on the porch light, but when she opens the door to step out for a look, a cold chill runs down her spine. She calls out for possibly one of the kids but sees and hears nothing. Again, this eerie wind-like feeling consumes her, so she turns to retreat back to the door, but as she does she is staring straight at long, sharp fangs — dripping with wolf saliva — coming for her throat.

As the fangs rip out her jugular veins, she grabs a handful of white fur as a final souvenir because it is the last thing her withered hands will ever touch. A small part of human frame was all that could be dragged inside. Lights went out and doors were pulled closed. Not having any relatives in the states and being a Japanese person that didn't own a car, she was not missed for a long time.

Once the four creatures had their fill of human flesh, they scurried back on the mountain to howl for hours at their triumphant conquer.

Things back at the colony were very busy, and Alexandru commanded everyone to transform, pair off, and mate for as long as they wanted. Copulating and howling uncontrollably was a ghastly and demonic sight. Birth control was distributed so no girl would get pregnant. Alexandru was so consumed with his desires that he wanted everyone to be that way, even though it was such an unnatural human behavior. The three natural killers were ruthless with this sadistic opportunity.

All these former sex slaves were actually worse off now than when they were having to deal with perverted prostitute buyers on the street. The only thing positive was they were being fed and housed lavishly. Sky and Moon were ordered to stay away from the dangerous three for their own safety. Hypnosis is a powerful thing for controlling a human being to make them do unimaginable suggestions.

Alexandru was developing a strong liking for Dawn, whom had a pure and sweet personality. She was very obedient to him and was seriously falling in love — her first. It was the only opportunity she ever had in her young, tormented life for this kind of emotional feeling.

MASACRE

Crystal Lake in the San Gabriel Mountains is the only naturally occurring lake in these mountains above the city of Azusa at 5,500 feet above sea level. It is a very popular hiking and camping park that's close to Los Angeles. This was the destination Alexandru picked to find more human prey. Waiting for someone to come along the trail would be easy as shooting Mallard ducks on a pond. He dives into his next midnight raid to feast.

Drinking the potion almost on a daily basis was changing Alexandru's brain more and more into this myth-like creature — a clinical for real wolf person. His taste for human flesh was becoming the most important craving inside him, even more than the sexual thing. He had to have human flesh and blood to survive, or so he thought. It was still the three natural born killers and himself that were afflicted by these urges, and the rest of his colony could not bring themselves to participate in human mutilation no matter how hard Alexandru tried — it just wasn't born in them.

Telling his three running mates that they were transforming that night to seek prey at Crystal Lake, the Russian tells Alexandru in his native tongue, "I would like for us to go to Russia because there are some leaders over there that I would love to rip their lungs out. The starvation and cruelty my mother, father, and family had to suffer was horrible."

The two from Uganda said the same thing about their family and country. "We could get so much revenge and satisfaction because as wolf creatures we would be able to stand our ground against the ruthless leadership we had to endure as children."

Alexandru could understand why they were natural born killers because of not knowing anything else in life. "Maybe we will go over to your homelands for this purpose," Alexandru half-heartedly tells them.

As the sun sinks low on the horizon, the vials are handed out. It would be howling time very soon, and once transformed, the four covered the distance in no time. Their speed was something to behold, and they never got winded from running or climbing. Soon, they were hidden in the bushes on the Crystal Lake trail. Within just a few minutes, a group of hikers came up the trail, which had a light here and there for night hiking. They were all equipped with walking sticks and flashlights, chatting and cracking jokes about the lake, teasing each other about whether it was haunted or not. Typical things people kid about when walking with friends at night in a forest. If they had only known this wasn't going to be a laughing matter very soon.

As the hikers got closer, one of the creatures howled because he got overly excited from the scent of human blood. The hikers grabbed each other in fright and uncontrollably tried talking at the same time.

"What the hell was that?" one asked.

"Was that a dog?" another said.

"I don't know, but I'm getting the flying monkeys out of here," the youngest hiker blurted.

Like rabbits fleeing down the trail they all scattered. This made the four wolf creatures even more excited because they liked nothing better than the "hunt." With this party of eleven people, the wolves were on fours in seconds, slashing and ripping the life out of them.

Hearing their screams, the rest of the hikers in a blind panic hit overdrive in different directions. Some crashed through the woods while others took to the lake. The fright from what was happening was to the point of heart failure. Limbs, briers, and thorns were tearing their bodies bad enough, but they felt no pain. Escaping was the only thing they could think about.

The four wolf creatures were preoccupied with gorging on flesh and didn't realize the other seven hikers were getting away, so like white streaks of lightning, they picked up the trails and chased four more hikers down. Within moments, they were ripping more flesh and bones.

With luck finally on the side of the remaining hikers, they came to a small parking area where one camper was pulling out in his car. Screaming and crying uncontrollably, a girl and two boys jumped into the car before the driver knew why.

"Please get us out of here!" they all blurted out. "All the rest of our family and friends have been slaughtered up on the trail!"

That's all the driver needed to hear. He tears out of the parking area and stomps the gas pedal to the floor heading to the Ranger station six miles away.

The three hikers are all trying to explain at the same time to the ranger who tries calming them down enough to get the story. Finally, he pieces together what they had just experienced as best he can, not fully understanding exactly what they are trying to explain. The ranger decides to call in the sheriff and another forest ranger to meet him at the parking lot the camper left out from.

The ranger tells the scared out of their brains hikers to wait at the station until he returns to file a report and bandage up their bleeding arms and legs with a first aid kit. Off he goes to find out exactly what happened, thinking grizzly bear or mountain lion.

Meeting up with the other ranger, they pack rifles, flashlights, and long-range walkie talkies to communicate as they cautiously go up the trail looking for signs of a wild animal. The wolf creatures hear the two rangers approaching their kill area, and silently hide to get ready to strike again.

The two rangers are totally preoccupied looking for signs of some wild bear or cat and suddenly are attack by four vicious wolf creatures. One ranger with walkie talkie in hand screams to the station, "Help!" All three hikers hear that desperate cry which makes them much more hysterical than before.

The sheriff and his deputy come quickly into the station and listen to everything the hikers have experienced. When told about the two ranger's last radio transmission for help, the sheriff makes an uncomfortable decision to hold off for a few more hours till daybreak. He knows he needs more manpower for this situation because something doesn't jell in his deductions with a creepy feeling running down his back. He calls the station for more policemen to be at the Ranger Station at 6 am sharp and bring plenty of weapons for any situation that they may encounter.

As the time to move on the trail arrives, the sheriff and eight policemen start their search up the hiking trail. They come with dogs and weapons not knowing what to expect, but soon they discover the most ghastly sight any one of them had ever seen. All that was left of the two rangers were pieces of flesh, bloody bones, and ripped clothes. The human flesh was lying all over the kill area on the ground and in the bushes. The stench was horrendous, and one policeman puked his guts out from the odor.

The sheriff knew there were eight more people out there somewhere. About an hour in, the dogs find the first four that were slaughtered but took almost all day to locate the last four.

"This isn't from an animal attack," the sheriff explained.

It had to be more than one person was the conclusion of the policemen.

"What kind of psychotic person or persons could do such a thing, and for what reason?" the sheriff said, desperately.

"It's borderline cannibalistic," says one policeman.

Calling for paramedics and cleanup crews, the sheriff wanted a forensic expert to go over the crime scene with a fine-tooth comb.

"I don't want anything to be overlooked because I've never seen such an unnatural killing area like this," he says.

It was a heck of a job identifying the remains of all the people, and the forensics took two weeks to start a determination of what happened. Fangs and claws were the weapons of bringing lives to an end, but footprints were almost null and void because of the hard ground and "furry" feet. Not a fingerprint could be lifted because of the same reason — fur covered fingers with claws.

Psychiatrists were called on to help study the kind of personality it took to do such a thing. Everyone involved with this case had no answers. Could an animal not native to these parts be the culprit?

The news media got word and — brother — was the front page plastered with this hot news item. Alexandru reading all about it knew he had to lay low for a while, and he was freaking out that someone would discover his colony.

After weeks of digging, the sheriff couldn't come up with the first clue on the now called Crystal Lake massacre. The local FBI office in Los Angeles had been briefed on this puzzling case, so they contact the sheriff in charge to give him support if he wanted it. He responds by telling the agency, "I'll keep that in mind."

WOLF AND SPIDER

Weeks go by and the massacre slowly becomes a cold case. Scared people in the entire region are wanting answers, afraid to go out at night, and businesses are hurting financially, which creates an even bigger problem. The police department is under tremendous pressure, so the sheriff picks up the phone, calls the L.A. FBI Agency and says, "Okay, I need some help and the best you can supply. If I don't tell the people something, I won't be elected sheriff again!"

It didn't take the FBI Agency two minutes to know exactly whom to call. The Nashville department's phone rang, and the secretary says, "May I help you," very politely.

"This is Agent Black from the Los Angeles department, and I need to speak with Chief Johnson, please. It is of the utmost importance," he explains.

"Sure thing, one moment," she replies.

L.J. gets on the phone and snaps, "Black, you ole son of a gun, how in the world are you doing? It's been a long time, buddy."

Anxiously, Black explains, "I'm good my friend, but I got to go straight to something that has shaken the whole San Gabriel area and it's bad."

Explaining all that happened he says, "I need your Black Recluse to come to L.A. as soon as possible. We have a desperate situation that, in my opinion, he is the best answer for, for this whole community."

L.J tells him he had already heard of the situation out there.

Realizing the scope of this unexplained problem, L.J. tells Agent Black that he will have the Black Recluse and his helpers on a plane that night.

"I'll have to request a cargo plane to transport all the equipment the Recluse and crew will need. You can supply helicopter support," says Chief L.J.

Around six o'clock central standard time, B.R., Bob Jarvis (best undercover agent), and five more lawmen leave out of Nashville International Airport to

Los Angeles, California. They all were briefed on this unordinary crime investigation.

As B.R. gazes down on the clouds below, he tries piecing together these killings on what or who did them. At this point in time, even B.R. with his advanced mental reasoning hasn't come up with any logical explanation for what went down at Crystal Lake. The mystery of it all makes him that much more excited to dive into this unknown situation, even more than chasing down bank robbers. There is something about it that B.R. considers being on the unnatural list.

As they land, Agent Black meets his counterparts and asked, "Which one is the special agent?"

B.R. disguised as another tourist sticks out his hand and says, "Hello, I'm the one that's called B.R." Black told him how glad he was to meet him and that he was here to help.

"I have this gut feeling we are combating something never before experienced," Black says.

"You mean like a crazy person?" Bob Jarvis asked.

"I'm not sure," says Black.

They all are escorted to a hotel for the night, but with a large truck to use, they will go to San Gabriel Valley the next morning. A building had already been leased to work out their plans.

B.R. had shipped his Harley cycle and his dirt bike he used in the Amazon because with its silent muffler it could make a difference in certain situations.

Once everyone was settled in the valley building, they gathered for a plan of action, and meeting with the sheriff and park rangers was first on the list. Going over forensics was a must-do.

The next morning, B.R., Jarvis, and the agents drove the truck to the Ranger station where they met with the sheriff and chief forest ranger. B.R. had changed into another disguise and didn't say very much. He let Agent Jarvis do most of the talking.

As the sheriff described the death scenes, chills ran over the FBI Agents, but it only fired up the Recluse. Once again, him being a creature-of-the-night, his venom-pumped heart was beating over-time. What on earth could have done such a thing, his brain was trying to absorb.

They were taken to the crime scene that was still sealed off, and no one had used the trail ever since the massacre. People were too scared to use any of the park, and it had become a financial disaster with no end in sight.

As B.R. walked around the kill zone, he started picking up signals he had never felt before. "Nothing is adding up here," he thought. Exactly what, he still wasn't sure why. His brain kept trying to calculate that it was something not native to this planet. With a chuckle he said, "We may be dealing with someone or something from outer space."

Back at the lodging in the valley, B.R. says, "Let's do some old fashioned police work."

He tells Bob and the agents to hit the back streets to start asking questions about both the valley and even L.A.

"Try to come up with anything we might associate with why or what had happened at Crystal Lake." B.R. orders.

The next few days, the agents walk the streets and bar rooms seeking any kind of information on the massacre or just anything unusual around the area. Finally, Agent Jarvis — sitting and having a beer and trying to appear as a barfly — overhears a real old barfly talking in Spanish to this half-drunk female sitting at the bar. She finally tells him to beat it because she wasn't interested. Jarvis walks over to him, laughs, and in Spanish says, "Too bad, man, maybe better luck next time."

The old Mexican thanks him and says, "Buy you some tequila."

They shoot the breeze for a little while and the old man asked, "What are you doing here if you came from Nashville?"

Bob tells him he is a reporter from a big newspaper trying to find out information on the Crystal Lake massacre.

By then, the old Mexican is getting polluted, and since Bob speaks his language so good, he leans over to impress him and says, "I know something that no one else knows about that subject."

Bob's ears perk up and said he says, "Oh really, just what do you happen to know? And if you talk right, I'll buy you tequila."

"Promise you won't tell I told you, but I heard while down in Mexico that some dude has a colony up in the mountains from the valley and strange things — unnatural — go on there," the old barfly revealed.

"Bingo," thinks Bob Jarvis.

"There's all kinds of religious freaks out here in California," barfly explains.

"Probably another form of a religious denomination," Agent Jarvis said.

After one more round, the FBI Agent says, "I better leave while I can still drive. Nice to meet you and have a nice day." He walks back to a motel room to spend the night and sober up.

Soon as he gets back to the valley building, he hands B.R. a map of the San Gabriel area. He explains what he learned from the Mexican and how this information is linked to the massacre with his gut feeling.

B.R. tells Bob, "You may just be on to something. Let's get a chopper in the air, pronto." B.R.'s eyes widen and he shakes Bob's hand saying, "Good work, my man."

Bob thanks him and as he does, he thinks to himself, "Damn, his grip is like a bear trap."

With a chopper it doesn't take long for B.R. to locate the old shack. He calls agent Black and tells him to fly close to the directions he gave him and take photographs. Make it look as though you're just passing over to land at the local airport.

Next day, the photos are developed and B.R. tells Jarvis to get his dirt bike ready because that night, the Black Recluse is going on the prowl. The photographs show people coming and going into an opening which is the mine shaft. He puts two and two together and begins to suspect there's more going on there than religion. His bulletproof outfit is taken out of its safe-like hanger.

About seven that evening finds B.R. easing around behind the mine shaft. He parks his bike close to a rock embankment and moves silently through some bushes and gets close to the colonists that are browsing and chatting with one another. They are completely unaware of his presence and one young teenage girl comes close to the Recluse crouched behind a large rock. Before she even knows anything, a gloved hand is over her mouth, and she is carried far enough back so that he can interrogate her without being heard by the others.

The young girl is sedated daily with heroin but, having used it for so long, it doesn't have a lot of effect anymore. The Recluse assures her he is a friend so not to be afraid.

"Easy for you to say," she says while looking at his outfit with the huge spider.

"I am here to set you free and I'm guessing you are here not of your free will," he said.

This girl isn't surprised by anything after all she's been through in her young life.

"Okay, what do you want from me? Because everyone wants something from me." she says.

The Recluse explains to her about the Crystal Lake incident and wants to know if she can tell him anything about it.

Taking a difficult chance with this stranger she asked him, "Will you really take me away from this colony?"

He had noticed she had a chain on her legs, so he says, "Stand up and let me take that chain off you."

The Recluse places the chain on a rock and puts his foot on it while taking the rest of the chain in his hand. With one jerk, he snaps the chain in two and then says, "Yes, you're going to leave this place. Just tell me if you know anything that isn't right about the colony."

She takes a deep breath and explains that werewolves had killed the people.

"What the H---, heck are you saying, young lady?" stammers the Recluse.

"Honest to God, it's true," she said.
Puzzled and confused, the Recluse says, "Alright, let's get you out of here before someone misses you." He sticks out his hand and introduces himself. "I'm the Black Recluse."

She replies, "I'm Amanda."

He sits her behind him on the bike and silently travels back to the valley building. After feeding her and making her comfortable, he tells Jarvis to find medication to detox her from heroin.

The Recluse says, "Now, what did you say about werewolves? Don't you know that's just a myth? Girl you must really believe what you are saying, but someone has really got you mixed up."

Amanda says, "Let me start from the beginning."

All the agents sit around and can't wait to hear this story, something modern history had never heard.

The Recluse, still in his uniform, says, "You have the floor, young lady."

She starts at the beginning of her early life and tells of how she was kidnapped and placed into human trafficking all the way up to where she was bought by the Romanian Alexandru Nicolae. How he had built the mine pods, shack, and colony. The most important piece of information was how he created a chemical potion that could transform a human into a wolf creature. She continues with every piece of information on this long period of the colony and inhabitants.

The FBI Agents are staring at her in almost total disbelief.

Agent Jarvis asked her, "Are you sure of these facts and is there any reason you would make any of this up? This is something Hollywood couldn't come up with."

She asked him what his name was and said, "Mr. Jarvis, you're the FBI, so you tell me what you think happened at Crystal Lake if you're so smart."

The Recluse steps in and with those sixth senses says, "What Amanda is laying out is not made up. I could tell if she were lying. Tell me something I need to know, Amanda. Are the four flesh eaters going to transform into wolf creatures anytime soon?"

"In about two hours, they will be hunting animal prey east of the colony — because of the massacre, they are laying low for a while on human prey," she explains.

"Tell me exactly how they will leave the colony," the Recluse says.

"They will leave out the back door of the shack, and there's a full moon. You can't miss them because they are solid white," Amanda said.
"Thank you, young lady, and that's all I need to know. I don't want any other colonists to get in the crossfire," the Recluse states.

With an automatic rifle and a machete on the side of his dirt bike, the Recluse blazes up toward the colony to introduce himself to some wolf creatures. He gives out a little chuckle and thinks back to when he jokingly said he would fight a pack of werewolves. Little did he know that joke was a reality for him. He had never been so pumped in his life.

As he rode, he thought it was going to be a significant test for the Black Recluse. Were the wolf creatures clinically human wolf people or were they invincible, created as a Devil's pawn? One way to find out, he contemplated.

As he silently motored his way around the colony and up behind a hill, he sneaks as close to the back door of the shack as he can. Watching the moon appear as the sun slides toward the western horizon, he knows they will come roaring out very soon according to Amanda.

With rifle in one hand and machete in the other, he watches the door from behind a cluster of bushes. Laying the machete down and reaching into a small bag, he pulls out a can that Jarvis had purchased earlier at a novelty store. It was a can of skunk smelling spray. When the Recluse was told of werewolves by Amanda, he sent Jarvis to quickly pick this item up for him.

He sprayed the skunk spray toward the back door so it would confuse the wolf creatures' sense of smell. He knew they could smell him, so he hoped the spray would work. A gamble that did work out for him.

The back door swung open and out came the three natural born killers. The Recluse fired six bullets into the first one out and it answered his question. They were human-made wolf creatures. As the bullets hit, down fell the first wolf man, but he managed to get back up. He wasn't moving very fast, but still moving.

This alerted the other three and Alexandru stopped and watched the battle from the doorway. He had figured that sooner or later the cops would find out about his colony. It was inevitable after all the press releases in the newspapers about Crystal Lake. He just didn't know it would be someone glowing like a ghost in an unidentified costume.

The other two wolf creatures were on the Black Recluse so quickly it surprised him.

"Okay, it's showtime!" he yelled loudly.

As the two wolf creatures circle to each side of him, he points the machete at each one's face and says, "You want some of this?"

The two wolf men give a long howl and then attack, but to their surprise, he is quicker than they are. Moving and slashing his machete, it catches one across the shoulder which leaves a deep gash.

"Well you do bleed, huh?" the Recluse says.

The two wolves become more angry and aggressive, clawing and snapping their fangs close to the Recluse's face. The claws leave deep scratches on his suit, but can't penetrate. In a lightning move, the Recluse is behind one and splits his skull open with his machete. As he drops to the ground growling in agony, the other one latches onto the Recluse, clawing and trying to bite his neck with his fangs.

To the wolf creature's dismay, their claws and fangs cannot penetrate his space age type steel the suit is made of, even though they are rattlesnake fast and super strong. Problem was the wolf creatures have never challenged a man that is supercharged with venom blood. His strength and speed were very superior.

It still was a vicious fight to the death, and when they could keep the Black Recluse occupied wrapped around his body, he was unable to accurately use his weapons. The only thing he had in one hand was the machete.

The first wolf creature whom the Recluse shot managed to limp to him and wrap around his leg. The only thing unprotected was the Recluse's face, and the wolf creatures knew it. When they tried ripping his face, the Recluse with awesome strength, would latch onto a limb and throw the wolf person through the air, but back again he would come.

The colonists were watching this historic battle from a distance, and they didn't have any idea who the Black Recluse was, but secretly they were pulling for him.

The wolf creature with the split skull with brains oozing out was desperately trying to help out. The Recluse reached down to the one on his leg, wrapped his hand around his neck, and with unbelievable power, squeezed his neck down to the size of a string bean, and with a jerk snapped the wolf's head completely off.

By then, the fight had lasted forever so it seemed. Claws, fangs, and machete were slashing and snapping in every direction. Just as fast as the Recluse threw the wolf man off, he was back slashing again and trying to hit his face. On the last throw off, the wolf creature came growling back, but this time the Recluse caught him in midair. He timed it just right with one hand in the wolf's hand and the other hand in the wolf's other hand. They stood toe to toe with hands locked together — the trial of strength was about to determine who was superior.

Looking each other eye to eye, the power struggle began. Both pushed back as the colonists began cheering. Slowly, the mighty Black Recluse started bending the wolf creature's wrists back, and with a strength indescribable, he snapped the wolf's wrists in half and with a mighty jerk ripped his hands and claws from his arms. The wolf creature was doing some howling now.

The Recluse raised his boot and kicked him back to where Alexandru was watching. Taking out his trusty double barrel shotgun, the Recluse walks up to the handless wolf creature, points it at his face and blows his head to kingdom come. Hearing the last one growl, whose skull was split, the Recluse reaches for his machete and — whack — off goes his head.

"Just wanted to put you out of your misery," says the Recluse.

He then turns and, with shotgun reloaded, walks up to the wolf creature Alexandru and snarls, "Are you the idiot Romanian that has almost destroyed this whole community and for what, sexual pleasure? You are the worst piece of cow turd I have ever witnessed. I'm really a lover myself, that's why I'm going to kiss this shotgun before I blow the great Alexandru Nicolae's head to Hell."

As he pulls the hammers back, Alexandru says, "Wait, I want to say something."

The Recluse replies, "I didn't know wolf creatures could talk, only howl."

"We can't under the spell, but I can, so let me tell you why," said Alexandru.

"I knew this day would come, and I'm glad. I'm growing weary because the potion I created is taking its toll on me. I have just swallowed enough arsenic poison to kill ten men and that's why I can speak. The potion is wearing off and I'm dying. There is a girl named Dawn and I want you to take care of her and all the other colonists. It wasn't their fault. I love Dawn, the only woman I've ever told. Would you tell me who you are?" pleads Alexandru.

"Umm, don't think I have any sympathy for you because I don't. What you've done is beyond evil. I will take care of these poor tortured souls you have abused," says the Recluse.

He turns and asked for the girl named Dawn. She walks toward them and says, "I am Dawn."

The Recluse said, "This beast that once was a man still has enough compassion left to feel love for the first time in his life, and that tiny ounce of love is for you. I think he wants you to move on with your life once he's gone and he's going now.

"To answer your last question, Mr. Nicolae, I'm a ghost returned from the grave to fight men like you, but you can call me the Black Recluse and I will return every time someone like you threatens another man's life," he states.

The poison causes Alexandru to transform back to human, and as he struggles to breathe, Dawn crying says," I will always love you. Goodbye."

With that said, Alexandru succumbs to death as tears roll down Dawn's face.

With a call to Agent Jarvis, the truck is headed to pick up the colonists. The Recluse searches and finds all of Alexandru's papers and tapes. Just so no one will ever know how to create wolf monsters again, the Recluse burns them all.

After six months of hospitals and psychologists, the colonists are finally free and ready to start a new life. Dawn asked Chief L.J. if she could go to school and become an FBI Agent. Chief said it would be an honor to have her.

B.R. sits down in L.J.'s office and laughs, "Me and my big mouth about werewolves, geez! Better be careful what you ask for!"

With that said, the book is closed on wolves.

THE PHONE CALL

One night I got a phone call — a number I didn't recognize. A man with a gruff voice asked for Bill. I told him it was the one and only.

He laughed and said, "You ole son-a-gun, how are you?"

Instantly, I recognized the voice of my long-time friend J.R. Dawkins.

188

"Why in the world are you calling me, big shot FBI Agent? You can't arrest me because you can't catch me," I smirked.

After catching up on a few years of not seeing each other,

J.R. said he needed me to meet him at one of our old stomping grounds in Kantrell Crossing and come alone.

We met and I was floored at how big and tough he looked.

"I have something I need to talk with you about because outside of the Agency, you are only one of a handful that knows my secret of spider venom," J.R. explains.

I told him, "Yes, and it goes no further than me."

J.R. told me, "Here's my dilemma. Can you tell me if you think I have aged?"

Looking at him closely I honestly thought he looked the same as he did when I saw him last, only more muscular.

"No, you don't look any older. Is it the venom, I speculate?"

Yeah, I just don't know how to deal with it," he confessed.

"Well I know you won't give up the venom, and nobody wants to grow old, so just look at it as a blessing," I said.

"Umm, I guess you're right, but it's something I'll have to accept, and it might become complicated," he says.

TO BE CONTINUED

www.ingramcontent.com/pod-product-compliance
Lightning Source LLC
Chambersburg PA
CBHW072134170626
46813CB00004BA/1558